The Two Sams

The Two Sams

Ghost Stories

GLEN HIRSHBERG

CARROLL & GRAF PUBLISHERS
NEW YORK

THE TWO SAMS
GHOST STORIES

Carroll & Graf Publishers
An Imprint of Avalon Publishing Group Inc.
161 William St., 16th Floor
New York, NY 10038

For Kim and Sid and Kate, with ghosts and places to go back to

And for my students, who demanded these stories, and
inspired many more. With love, from the man with the Jell-O

Any resemblance to places living or dead is sort of coincidental

Introduction

Sometimes just one book can be enough to confirm the presence of a major talent in the field of the supernatural tale. If M. R. James had published only *Ghost Stories of an Antiquary,* Fritz Leiber *Night's Black Agents,* or Thomas Ligotti *Songs of a Dead Dreamer,* they would certainly each be guaranteed a secure place in the pantheon. I'm not wishing for an instant that the present book prove to be Glen Hirshberg's sole collection, but I'll stake my reputation that history will hail him as a crucial contributor to the field. With a writer of his talents to bear the tradition into the new century, it's in no danger of becoming irrelevant.

With very few exceptions (Lovecraft and Leiber come immediately to mind) the best work in the genre has emerged from literature, not the pulps. Hirshberg's certainly does. He brings enviable skills to his work: a stylistic precision that comes of loving language, an unerring eye for character and the moments that define or reveal it, a keen sense not just of place but how light and the time of day transform his settings. It's his sense of the spectral, however, that puts him up there with the best. In this book it informs and underlies five of the most haunting recent tales in the field.

This said, the stories seldom deal with the merely ghostly. While "Struwwelpeter" is beset by it—not least in an abandoned house so variously restless it's close to becoming a spectre in itself—the tale reminds us how adolescence could be full of small everyday terrors, and not all the characters survive. Like most of the contents, this story is a novella, a form often thought to be ideal for the genre. It also allows Hirshberg the space to make his situations real.

His concern for young people out on some edge of themselves reappears in "Shipwreck Beach." We may reflect that Hirshberg is a teacher; somebody in every tale is one. Some of the characters these teachers are involved with choose to be beyond their or anybody's help. This story conjures up a Hawaiian landscape that borders on the numinous, while the mysterious finale suggests a myth so ancient it's past identification. The foundation of the story and of its fellows is their moral sense. Too often, when the supernatural story turns moral it just takes dusty puppets representing good and evil out of their box and bangs them together until the evil one falls down, but Hirshberg's vision is too clear and rigorous to settle for cliché. Nor does he preach, thank God.

"Mr. Dark's Carnival" makes explicit a theme that others of the stories touch on: the allure of terror. It goes so far as to find a redemptive power in spectral excitement, but things aren't so simple; indeed, in Hirshberg's work they never are. It's the second of these tales to celebrate Halloween. His inventiveness is admirably demonstrated by the way he reimagines that ghostly night in both—no repetition there. The story presents a carnival exhibition as unconventional as it is (very) disturbing, not least because the spectral isn't confined to it. Often in Hirshberg one senses it everywhere.

I believe "Dancing Men" was written in response to a request by the esteemed anthologist Ellen Datlow for ghost story writers to scare her. I had a go myself, but this tale goes much further. It faces the worst human beings can do to one another and to themselves, and reaches conclusions more lasting and more devastating than any scare. Though it has recourse to myth, that isn't reassuring either. "Grow up," the narrator is told, an exhortation that resonates through all these stories, but neither the process nor its outcome is comfortable. I'd call that truth to life.

Perhaps the title story offers consolation after we have lived through some of the most harrowing experiences in the book. I hope nobody need wonder why the author read it aloud to his students only once. Like other tales here, it's a good deal more moving than conventional expectations of the genre would anticipate. Central to it is the notion that terror comes with simply living. Tales like these help give it shape and contribute insights into it. They certainly also provide the aesthetic experience only ghost stories can furnish. Glen Hirshberg is true to his own experience and to the best of his field. May he continue to enrich it and develop it. He's an original and a considerable talent, and I'm proud to be associated with his book.

Ramsey Campbell
Wallasey, Merseyside
8 May 2003

Struwwelpeter

"The dead are not altogether powerless."

—Chief Seattle

This was before we knew about Peter, or at least before we understood what we knew, and my mother says it's impossible to know a thing like that, anyway. She's wrong, though, and she doesn't need me to tell her she is, either, as she sits there clutching her knees and crying in the television light.

Back then, we still gathered after-school afternoons at the Anderszs' house because it was close to the locks. If it wasn't raining, we'd drop our books and grab Ho Hos out of the tin Mr. Andersz always left on the table for us and head immediately toward the water. Gulls spun in the sunlight overhead, their cries urgent, taunting, telling us, *you're missing it, you're missing it.* We'd sprint between the rows of low stone duplexes, the sad little gardens with their flowers battered by the rain until the petals looked bent and forgotten like discarded training wheels, the splintery, sagging blue walls of the Black Anchor Restaurant where Mr. Paars used to hunker alone and murmuring over his plates of reeking lutefisk when he wasn't stalking Market Street, knocking pigeons and homeless people out of the way with his dog-head cane. Finally, we'd burst into the park and pour down the avenue of fir trees like a mudslide, scattering people, bugs, and birds before us until we hit the water.

For hours, we'd prowl the green hillsides, watching the sailors yell at the invading seals from the top of the locks while the seals ignored them, skimming for fish and sometimes rolling on their backs and flipping their fins. We watched the rich-people sailboats with their masts rusting, the big gray fishing boats from Alaska and Japan and Russia with the fishermen bored on deck, smoking, throwing butts at the seals and leaning on the rails while the gulls shrieked overhead. As long as the rain held off, we stayed and threw stones to see how high up the opposing bank we could get them, and Peter would wait for ships to drift in front of us and then throw low over their bows. The sailors would scream curses in other languages or sometimes ours, and Peter would throw bigger stones at the boat hulls. When they hit with a thunk, we'd flop on our backs on the wet grass and flip our feet in the air like the seals. It was the rudest gesture we knew.

Of course, most days, it was raining, and we stayed in the Anderszs' basement until Mr. Andersz and the Serbians came home. Down there, in the damp—Mr. Andersz claimed his was one of three basements in all of Ballard—you could hear the wetness rising in the grass outside like lock water. The first thing Peter did when we got downstairs was flick on the gas fire-place—not for heat, it didn't throw any—and we'd toss in stuff: pencils, a tinfoil ball, a plastic cup, and once a broken old 45 which formed blisters on its surface and then spit black goo into the air like a fleeing octopus dumping ink before it slid into a notch in the logs to melt. Once, Peter went upstairs and came back with one of Mr. Andersz's red spiral photo albums and tossed it into the flames, and when one of the Mack sisters asked him what was in it, he told her, "No idea. Didn't look."

The burning never lasted long, five minutes, maybe. Then we'd eat Ho Hos and play the Atari Mr. Andersz had bought Peter years before at a yard sale, and it wasn't like you think, not always. Mostly, Peter flopped in his orange beanbag chair with his long legs stretched in front of him and his too-long black bangs splayed across his forehead. He let me and the Mack sisters take turns on the machine, and Kenny London and Steve Rourke, too, back in the days when they used to come. I was the best at the basic games, Asteroids and Pong, but Jenny Mack could stay on Dig Dug forever and not get grabbed by the floating grabby things in the ground. Even when we asked Peter to take his turn, he wouldn't. He'd say, "Go ahead," or "Too tired," or "Fuck off," and once I even turned around in the middle of losing to Jenny and found him watching us, sort of, the rainy window and us, not the TV screen at all. He reminded me a little of my grandfather before he died, all folded up in his chair and not wanting to go anywhere and kind of happy to have us there. Always, Peter seemed happy to have us there.

When Mr. Andersz got home, he'd fish a Ho Ho out of the tin for himself if we'd left him one—we tried to, most days—and then come downstairs, and when he peered out of the stairwell, his black wool hat still stuck to his head like melted wax, he already looked different than when we saw him at school. At school, even with his hands covered in yellow chalk and his transparencies full of fractions and decimals scattered all over his desk and the pears he carried with him and never seemed to eat, he was just Mr. Andersz, fifth-grade math teacher, funny accent, funny to get angry. At school, it never occurred to any of us to feel sorry for him.

"Well, hello, all of you," he'd say, as if talking to a litter of puppies he'd found, and we'd pause our game and hold our breaths and wait for Peter. Sometimes—most times—Peter said, "Hey" back, or even "Hey, Dad." Then we'd all chime in like a clock tolling the hour, "Hey, Mr. Andersz," "Thanks for the Ho Hos," "Your hat's all wet again," and he'd smile and nod and go upstairs.

There were the other days, too. A few, that's all. On most of those, Peter just didn't answer, wouldn't look at his father. It was only the one time that he said, "Hello, Dipshit Dad," and Jenny froze at the Atari and one of the floating grabby things swallowed her digger, and the rest of us stared—but not at Peter, and not at Mr. Andersz, either. Anywhere but there.

For a few seconds, Mr. Andersz seemed to be deciding. Rivers of rain wriggled down the walls and windows like transparent snakes, and we held our breath. But all he said in the end was,

"We'll talk later, Struwwelpeter," which was only a little different from what he usually said when Peter got this way. Usually, he said, "Oh. It's you, then. Hello, Struwwelpeter." I never liked the way he said that, as though he was greeting someone else entirely, not his son. Eventually, Jenny or her sister Kelly would say, "Hi, Mr. Andersz," and he'd glance around at us as though he'd forgotten we were there. Then he'd go upstairs and invite the Serbians in, and we wouldn't see him again until we left.

The Serbians made Steve Rourke nervous, which, tonight, is almost funny, in retrospect. They were big and dark, both of them, two brothers who looked at their hands whenever they saw children. One was a car mechanic, the other worked at the locks, and they sat all afternoon, most afternoons, in Mr. Andersz's study, sipping tea and speaking Serbian in low whispers. The words made their whispers harsh, full of z's and ground-up s's, as though they'd swallowed glass. "They could be planning things in there," Steve used to say. "My dad says both those guys were badass soldiers." Mostly, as far as I could tell, they looked at Mr. Andersz's giant library of photo albums and listened to records. Judy Collins, Joan Baez. Almost funny, like I said.

Of course, by this last Halloween—my last night at the Andersz house—both Serbians were dead, run down by a drunken driver while walking across Fremont Bridge, and Kenny London had moved away, and Steve Rourke didn't come anymore. He said his parents wouldn't let him, and I bet they wouldn't, but that isn't why he stopped coming. I knew it, and I think Peter knew it, too, and that worried me, a little, in ways I couldn't explain.

I almost didn't get to go, either. I was out the door, blinking in the surprising sunlight and the wind rolling off the Sound, when my mother yelled, *"Andrew!"* and stopped me. I turned to find her in the open screen door of our duplex, arms folded over the long gray coat she still wears inside and out from October to May, sunlight or no, graying curls bunched on top of her scalp as though trying to crawl over her head out of the wind. She seemed to be wiggling in midair like a salmon trying to hold itself still against a current. Rarely did she take what she called her "frustrations" out on me, but she'd been crabby all day, and now she looked furious, despite the fact that I'd stayed in my room out of her way from the second I got home from school, because I knew she didn't really want me out tonight. Not with Peter. Not after last year.

"That's a costume?" She gestured with her chin at my jeans, my everyday black sweater, too-small brown mac she'd promised to replace this year.

I shrugged.

"You're not going trick-or-treating?"

The truth was, no one went trick-or-treating much in our section of Ballard, not like in Bellingham, where we'd lived when we lived with my dad. Too wet and dismal, most years, and there were too many drunks lurking around places like the Black Anchor and sometimes stumbling down the duplexes, shouting curses at the dripping trees.

"Trick-or-treating's for babies," I said.

"Hmm, I wonder which of your friends taught you that," my mother said, and then a look flashed across her face, different from the one she usually got at times like this. She still looked sad, but not about me. She looked sad *for* me. The same way she looks right now.

I took a step toward her, and her image wavered in my glasses. "I won't sleep there. I'll be home by eleven," I said.

"You'll be home by ten, or you won't be going anywhere again anytime soon. Got it? How old do you think you are, anyway?"

"Twelve," I said, with as much conviction as I could muster, and my mother flashed the sad look again.

"If Peter tells you to jump off a bridge . . ."

"Push him off."

My mother nodded. "If I didn't feel so bad for *him* . . ." I thought she meant Peter, and then I wasn't sure. But she didn't say anything else, and after a few seconds, I couldn't stand there anymore, not with the wind crawling under the neck of my jacket and my mother still looking like that. I left her in the doorway.

Even in bright sunlight, mine was a dreary neighborhood. The gusts of wind herded paper scraps and street grit down the overflowing gutters and yanked the last leaves off the trees like a gleeful gang on a vandalism rampage. I saw a few parents—new to the area, obviously—hunched into rain slickers, leading little kids from house to house. The kids wore drugstore clown costumes, Darth Vader masks, sailor caps. They all looked edgy and miserable. At most of the houses, no one answered the doorbell.

Outside the Anderszs' place, I stopped for just a minute, watching the leaves leaping from their branches like lemmings and tumbling down the wind, trying to figure out what was different, what felt wrong. Then I had it: The Mountain was out. The endless fall rain had rolled in early that year, and it had been weeks, maybe months, since I'd last seen Mount Rainier. Seeing it now gave me the same unsettled sensation as always. "It's because you're looking south, not west," people always say, as if that explains how the mountain gets to that spot on the horizon, on the wrong side of the city, not where it actually is but out to sea, seemingly bobbing on the waves, not the land.

How many times, I wondered abruptly, had some adult in my life asked why I liked Peter? They still ask, sometimes, even though we haven't hung around each other much the past few years, but back then, it was an everyday topic when the topic was me. I wasn't cruel, and despite my size, I wasn't easily cowed, and I did okay in school—not as well as Peter, but okay—and I had "a gentleness, most days," as Mrs. Corbett (WhoreButt, to Peter) had written on my report card last year. "If he learns to exercise judgment—and perhaps gives some thought to his choice of companions—he could go far."

I wanted to go far—from Ballard, anyway, and the locks and the smell of lutefisk and the rain. I liked doorbell ditching, but I didn't get much charge out of throwing stones through windows. And if people were home when we did it, came out and shook their fists, or worse, just stood there, looking at us the way you would at a wind or an earthquake, nothing you could slow or stop, I'd freeze, feeling bad, until Peter screamed at me or yanked me so hard that I had no choice but to follow.

I could say I liked how smart Peter was, and I did. He could sit dead still for twenty-seven minutes of a thirty-minute comprehension test, then scan it and answer every question right before the teacher, furious, hovering over him and watching the clock, could snatch the paper away without the rest of us screaming foul. He could recite the periodic table of elements backwards, complete with atomic weights. He could build skyscrapers five feet high out of chalk and rubber-cement jars and toothpicks and crayons that always stayed standing until anyone who wasn't him tried to touch them.

I could say I liked the way he treated everyone the same, which he did, in a way. He'd been the first in my grade—the only one, for a year or so—to hang out with the Mack sisters, who were still, at that point, the only African-Americans in our school. But he wasn't all that nice to the Macks, really. Just no nastier than he was to the rest of us.

No. I liked Peter for exactly the reason my mother and my

teachers feared I did: because he was fearless, because he was cruel—although mostly to people who deserved it when it wasn't Halloween—and most of all, because he really did seem capable of anything. So many of the people I knew seemed capable of nothing, for whatever reason. Capable of nothing.

Out on the whitecap-riddled Sound, the sun sank, and the Mountain turned red. It was like looking inside it and seeing it living. Shivering slightly in the wind, I hopped the Anderszs' three stone steps and rang the bell.

"Just come in, fuck!" I heard Peter yell from the basement. I started to open the door, and Mr. Andersz opened it for me. He had his gray cardigan straight on his waist for once and his black hat was gone and his black and gray hair was wet and combed on his forehead, and I had the awful, hilarious idea that he was going on a date.

"Andrew, come in," he said, sounding funny, too formal, the way he did at school. He didn't step back right away, though, and when he did, he put his hand against the mirror on the hallway wall, as though the house was rocking underneath him.

"Hey, Mr. Andersz," I said, wiping my feet on the shredded green mat that said something in Serbian. Downstairs, I could hear the burbling of the Dig Dug game, and I knew the Mack sisters had arrived. I flung my coat over Peter's green slicker on the coat rack, took a couple steps toward the basement door, turned around, and stopped.

Mr. Andersz had not moved, hadn't even taken his hand off the mirror, and now he was staring at it as though it was a spider frozen there.

"Are you all right, Mr. Andersz?" I asked, and he didn't respond. Then he made a sound, a sort of hiss, like a radiator when you switch it off.

"How many?" he muttered. I could barely hear him. "How

many chances? As a teacher, you know there won't be many. You get two, maybe three moments in an entire year. . . . Something's happened, there's been a fight or someone's sick or the soccer team won or something, and you're looking at a student . . ." His voice trailed off, leaving me with the way he said "student." He pronounced it stu-*dent*. It was one of the things we all made fun of, not mean fun, just fun. "You're looking at them," he said, "and suddenly, there they are. And it's *them*, and it's thrilling, terrifying, because you know you might have a chance. An opportunity. You can say something."

On the mirror, Mr. Andersz's hand twitched, and I noticed the sweat beading under the hair on his forehead. It reminded me of my dad, and I wondered if Mr. Andersz was drunk. Then I wondered if my dad was drunk, wherever he was. Downstairs, Jenny Mack yelled, "Get off" in her fighting voice, happy-loud, and Kelly Mack said, "Good, come on, this is *boring*."

"And as parent . . ." Mr. Andersz muttered. "How many? And what happens . . . the moment comes . . . but you're missing your wife. Just right then, just for a while. Or your friends. Maybe you're tired. It's just that day. It's rainy, you have meals to make, you're tired. . . . There'll be another moment. Surely. You have years. Right? You have years. . . ."

So fast and so silent was Peter's arrival in the basement doorway that I mistook him for a shadow from outside. I didn't even realize he was there until he pushed me in the chest. "What's your deal?" he said.

I started to gesture at Mr. Andersz, thought better of it, and shrugged. Footsteps clattered on the basement stairs, and then the Macks were in the room. Kelly had her tightly braided hair stuffed under a black, backward baseball cap. Her bare arms were covered in paste-on snake tattoos, and her face was dusted in white powder. Jenny wore a red sweater, black jeans. Her hair hung straight and shiny and dark, hovering just off her head and neck like a bird's crest, and I understood, for the first time, that she was pretty. Her eyes were bright green, wet and watchful.

"What are you supposed to be?" I said to Kelly, because suddenly I was uncomfortable looking at Jenny.

Kelly flung her arm out to point and did a quick, ridiculous shoulder wriggle. It was nothing like her typical movements; I'd seen her dance. "Vanilla Ice," she said, and spun around.

"Let's go," Peter said, stepping past me and his father and tossing my mac on the floor so he could get to his slicker.

"You want candy, Andy?" Jenny teased, her voice sing-songy.

"Ho Ho?" I asked. I was talking, I suppose, to Mr. Andersz, who was still staring at his hand on the mirror. I didn't want him to be in the way. It made me nervous for him.

The word "Ho Ho" seemed to rouse him, though. He shoved himself free of the wall, shook his head as if awakening, and said, "Just a minute," very quietly.

Peter opened the front door and let in the wind, and Mr. Andersz pushed it closed, not hard. But he leaned against it, and the Mack sisters stopped with their coats half on. Peter just stood beside him, his black hair sharp and pointy on his forehead like the tips of a spiked fence. But he looked more curious than angry.

Mr. Andersz lifted a hand to his eyes, squeezed them shut, opened them. Then he said, "Turn out your pockets."

Still, Peter's face registered nothing. He didn't respond to his father or glance at us. Neither Kelly nor I moved, either. Beside me, Jenny took a long, slow breath, as though she was clipping a wire on a bomb, and then she said, "Here, Mr. A," and she pulled the pockets of her black coat inside out, revealing two sticks of Dentyne, two cigarettes, a ring of keys with a Seahawks whistle dangling amongst them, and a ticket stub. I couldn't see what from.

"Thank you, Jenny," Mr. Andersz said, but he didn't take the cigarettes, hardly even looked at her. He watched his son.

Very slowly, after a long time, Peter smiled. "Look at you," he said. "Being daddy." He pulled out the liner of his coat pockets. There was nothing in them at all.

"Pants," said Mr. Andersz.

"What do you think you're looking for, Big Bad Daddy?" Peter asked. "What do you think you're going to find?"

"Pants," Mr. Andersz said.

"And what will you do, do you think, if you find it?" But he turned out his pants pockets. There was nothing in those, either, not even keys or money.

For the first time since Peter had come upstairs, Mr. Andersz looked at the rest of us, and I shuddered. His face looked the same way my mother's had when I left the house: a little scared, but mostly sad. Permanently, stupidly sad.

"I want to tell you something," he said. If he spoke like this in the classroom, I thought, no one would wedge unbent paper clips in his chalkboard erasers anymore. "I won't have it. There will be no windows broken. There will be no little children ter-rorized—"

"That wasn't our fault," said Jenny, and she was right, in a way. We hadn't known anyone was hiding in those bushes when we toilet-papered them, and Peter had meant to light his cigarette, not the roll of toilet paper.

"Nothing lit on fire. No one bullied or hurt. I won't have it, because it's beneath you, do you understand? You're the smartest children I know." Abruptly, Mr. Andersz's hands flashed out and grabbed his son's shoulders. "Do you hear me? You're the smartest child I've ever seen."

For a second, they just stood there, Mr. Andersz clutching Peter's shoulders as though trying to steer a runaway truck, Peter completely blank.

Then, very slowly, Peter smiled. "Thanks, Dad," he said.

"Please," Mr. Andersz said, and Peter opened his mouth, and we all cringed.

But what he said was, "Okay," and he slipped past his father and out the door. I looked at the Mack sisters. Together, we watched Mr. Andersz in the doorway with his head tilted forward on his neck and his hands tight at his sides, like a diver at the Olympics getting ready for a backflip. He never moved, though, and eventually we followed Peter out. I was last, and I thought I felt Mr. Andersz's hand on my back as I went by, but I wasn't sure, and when I glanced around, he was still just standing there, and the door swung shut.

I'd been inside the Andersz house fifteen minutes, maybe less, but the wind had chased the late-afternoon light over the horizon, and the Mountain had faded from red to dark gray, motionless now on the surface of the water like an oil tanker, one of those massive, passing ships on which no people were visible, ever. I've never liked my neighborhood, but back then I hated it after sundown, the city gone, the Sound indistinguishable from the black, starless sky, no one walking. It was like we were someone's toy set that had been closed up in its box and snapped shut for the night.

"Where are we going?" Kelly Mack asked, her voice sharp, fed up. She'd been sick of us, lately. Sick of Peter.

"Yeah," I said, rousing myself. I didn't want to soap car windows or throw rocks at street signs or put on rubber masks and scare trick-or-treaters, exactly, but those were the things we did. And we had no supplies.

Peter closed his eyes, leaned his head back, took a deep

breath of the rushing air and held it. He looked almost peaceful. I couldn't remember ever having seen him that way. It was startling. Then he stuck one trembling arm out in front of him, pointed at me, and his eyes sprung open.

"Do you know"—his voice was deep, accented, a perfect imitation—"what that bell does?"

I clapped my hands. "That bell," I said, in the closest I could get to the same voice, and the Mack sisters stared at us, baffled, which made me grin even harder, "raises the dead."

"What are you babbling about?" said Kelly to Peter, but Jenny was looking at me, seawater eyes curious and strange.

"You know Mr. Paars?" I asked her.

But of course she didn't. The Macks had moved here less than a year and a half ago, and I hadn't seen Mr. Paars, I realized, in considerably longer. Not since the night of the bell, in fact. I looked at Peter. His grin was as wide as mine felt. He nodded at me. We'd been friends a long time, I realized. Almost half my life.

Of course, I didn't say that. "A long time ago," I told the Macks, feeling like a longshoreman, a lighthouse keeper, someone with stories who lived by the sea, "there was this man. An old, white-haired man. He ate lutefisk—it's fish, it smells awful, I don't really know what it is—and stalked around the neighborhood, scaring everybody."

"He had this cane," Peter said, and I waited for him to go on, join me in the telling, but he didn't.

"All black," I said. "Kind of scaly. Ribbed, or something. It didn't look like a cane. And it had this silver dog's head on it, with fangs. A Doberman—"

"Anyway . . ." said Kelly, though Jenny seemed to be enjoying listening.

"He used to bop people with it. Kids. Homeless people.

Whoever got in his way. He stomped around Fifteenth Street terrorizing everyone. Two years ago, on the first Halloween we were allowed out alone, right about this time of night, Peter and I spotted him coming out of the hardware store. It's not there anymore, it's that empty space next to the place where the movie theater used to be. Anyway, we saw him there, and we followed him home."

Peter waved us out of his yard toward the locks. Again, I waited, but when he glanced at me, the grin was gone. His face was normal, neutral, maybe, and he didn't say anything.

"He lives down there," I said, gesturing to the south toward the Sound. "Way past all the other houses. Past the end of the street. Practically in the water."

Despite what Peter had said, we didn't head that way. Not then. We wandered toward the locks, into the park. The avenue between the pine trees was empty except for a scatter of solitary bums on benches, wrapping themselves in shredded jackets and newspapers as the night nailed itself down and the dark billowed around us in the gusts of wind like the sides of a tent. In the roiling trees, black birds perched on the branches, silent as gargoyles.

"There aren't any other houses that close to Mr. Paars," I said. "The street turns to dirt, and it's always wet because it's down by the water. There are these long, empty lots full of weeds, and a couple sheds. I don't know what's in them. Anyway, right where the pavement ends, Peter and I dropped back and just kind of hung out near the last house until Mr. Paars made it to his yard. Remember his yard, Peter?"

Instead of answering, Peter led us between the low stone buildings to the canal, where we watched the water swallow the last streaks of daylight like some monstrous whale gulping plankton. The only boats in the slips were two sailboats, sails furled, rocking as the waves slapped against them. The only person I saw on either stood at the stern of the boat closest to us, head hooded in a green oil slicker, face aimed out to sea.

"Think I could hit him from here?" said Peter, and I flinched and looked at his fists, expecting to see stones, but he was just asking. "Tell them the rest," he said.

I glanced at the Macks and was startled to see them holding hands, leaning against the rail over the canal, though they were watching us, not the water. "Finish the story, already," Kelly said, but Jenny just raised her eyebrows at me. Behind her, seagulls dipped and tumbled on the wind like shreds of cloud that had been ripped loose.

"We waited a while. It was cold. Remember how cold it was? We were wearing winter coats and mittens. It wasn't windy like this, but it was freezing. At least that made the dirt less muddy when we finally went down there. We passed the sheds and the trees, and there was no one—I mean no one—around. Too cold for any trick-or-treating anywhere around here, even if anyone was going to. And there wasn't anywhere to go on that street, anyway.

"It's all weird down there. Everything's flat, and then right as you get near the Paars place, this little forest springs up. Lots of thick firs. We couldn't really see anything."

"Except that it was light," Peter murmured.

"Yeah. Bright light. Mr. Paars had his yard floodlit, for burglars, we figured. We thought he was probably paranoid. So we snuck off the road when we got close and went into the trees. In there, it was wet. Muddy, too. My mom was so mad when I got home. I had pine needles sticking to me everywhere. She said I looked like I'd been tarred and feathered. We hid in this little grove, looked into the lawn, and we saw the bell."

Now Peter turned around, his hands flung wide to either side. "Biggest fucking bell you've ever seen in your life," he said.

"What are you talking about?" said Kelly.

"It was in this . . . pavilion," I started, not sure how to describe it. "Gazebo, I guess. All white and round, like a carousel, except the only thing inside was this giant white bell, like a church bell, hanging from the ceiling on a chain. And all the lights in the yard were aimed at it."

"Weird," said Jenny, leaning against her sister.

"Yeah. And that house. It's real dark, and real old. Black wood or something, all sort of falling apart. Two stories, kind of big. It looked like four or five of the sheds we passed sort of stacked on top of each other and squashed together. But the lawn was beautiful. Green, mowed perfectly, like a baseball stadium."

"Kind of," Peter whispered. He turned from the canal and wandered back between buildings down the tree-lined lane.

A shiver swept up the skin on my back as I realized, finally, why we were going back to the Paars house. I'd forgotten, until that moment, how scared we'd been. How scared Peter had been. Probably, Peter had been thinking about this for two years.

"It was so strange," I said to the Macks, all of us watching the bums in their paper blankets and the birds clinging by their talons to the branches and eyeing us as we passed. "All that outside light, the house falling apart and no lights on in there, no car in the driveway, that huge bell. So we just looked for a long time. Then, finally, we realized what was in the grass."

By now we were out of the park, back among the duplexes, and the wind had turned colder, though it wasn't freezing, exactly. In a way, it felt good, fresh, like a hard slap in the face.

"I want a shrimp-and-chips," Kelly said, gesturing over her shoulder toward Market Street, where the little fry stand still stayed open next to the Dairy Queen, although the Dairy Queen had been abandoned.

"I want to go see this Paars house," said Jenny. "Stop your

whining." She sounded cheerful, fierce, the way she did when she played Dig Dug or threw her hand in the air at school. She was smart, too—not Peter-smart, but as smart as me, at least. And I think she'd seen the trace of fear in Peter, barely there but suddenly visible, and it fascinated her. That's what I was thinking when she reached out casually and took my hand. Then I stopped thinking at all. "Tell me about the grass," she said.

"It was like a circle," I said, my fingers still, my palm flat against hers. Even when she squeezed, I kept still. I didn't know what to do, and I didn't want Peter to turn around. If Kelly had noticed, she didn't say anything. "Cut right in the grass. A pattern. A circle, with this upside-down triangle inside it, and—"

"How do you know it was upside down?" Jenny asked.

"What?"

"How do you know you were looking at it the right way?"

"Shut up," said Peter, quick and hard, not turning around, leading us onto the street that dropped down to the Sound, to the Paars house. Then he did turn around, and he saw our hands. But he didn't say anything. When he was facing forward again, Jenny squeezed once more, and I gave a feeble squeeze back.

We walked half a block in silence, but that just made me more nervous. I could feel Jenny's thumb sliding along the outside of mine, and it made me tingly, terrified. I said, "Upside down. Right side up. Whatever. It was a symbol, a weird one. It looked like an eye."

"Old dude must have had a hell of a lawn mower," Kelly muttered, glanced at Peter's back, and stopped talking, just in time, I thought. Mr. Andersz was right. She was smart, too.

"It kind of made you not want to put your foot in the grass," I continued. "I don't know why. It just looked wrong. Like it really could see you. I can't explain."

"Didn't make *me* want not to put my foot in the grass," Peter said.

I felt Jenny look at me. Her mouth was six inches or so from my hair, my ear. It was too much. My hand twitched and I let go. Blushing, I glanced at her. She looked surprised. Then she drifted away toward her sister.

"That's true," I said, wishing I could call Jenny back. "Peter stepped right out."

On our left, the last of the duplexes slid away, and we came to the end of the pavement. In front of us, the dirt road rolled down the hill, brown and wet and bumpy, like some giant cut-out tongue on the ground. I remembered the way Peter's duck boots had seemed to float on the surface of Mr. Paars's floodlit green lawn, as though he were walking on water.

"Hey," I said, though Peter had already stepped onto the dirt and was strolling, fast and purposeful, down the hill. "Peter," I called after him, though I followed, of course. The Macks were no longer near me. "When's the last time you saw him? Mr. Paars?"

He turned around, and he was smiling, now, the smile that scared me. "Same time you did, Bubba," he said. "Two years ago tonight."

I blinked, and the wind lashed me like the end of a twisted-up towel. "How do you know when I last saw him?" I said.

Peter shrugged. "Am I wrong?"

I didn't answer. I watched Peter's face, the dark swirling around and over it, shaping it, like rushing water over stone.

"He hasn't been anywhere. Not on Fifteenth Street. Not at the Black Anchor. Nowhere. I've been watching for him."

"Maybe he doesn't live there anymore," Jenny said carefully. She was looking at Peter, too.

"There's a car," Peter said. "A Lincoln. Long and black. Practically a limo."

"I've seen that car," I said. "I've seen it drive by my house right at dinnertime."

"It goes down there." Peter gestured toward the trees, the water, the Paars house. "Like I said, I've been watching."

And of course he had been, I thought. If his father had let him, he'd probably have camped right here, or in the gazebo under the bell. In fact, it seemed impossible to me, given everything I knew about Peter, that he'd let two years go by.

"Exactly what happened to you two down there?" Kelly asked.

"Tell them now," said Peter. "There isn't going to be any talking once we get down there. Not until we're finished." Dropping into a crouch, he picked at the cold, wet dirt with his fingers and watched the ferries drifting out of downtown toward Bainbridge Island. You couldn't really make out the boats from there, just the clusters of lights on the water like clouds of lost, doomed fireflies.

"The grass was way wet, too," I said, remembering the weight of my sopping pants against my legs. "I mean, everywhere was wet, as usual, but this was like wading in a pond. You put your foot down and the whole lawn rippled. It made the eye look like it was winking. At first we were kind of hunched over, sort of hiding, which was ridiculous in all that light. I didn't want to walk in the circle, but Peter just strolled right through it. He called me a baby because I went the long way around."

"I called you a baby because you were being one," Peter said, but not meanly, really.

"We kept expecting lights to go on in the house, or dogs to come out. It just seemed like there would be dogs. But there weren't. We got up to the gazebo, which was the only place in the whole yard with shadows because it was surrounded by all these trees. Bizarre trees. They were kind of stunted. Not pines, either, they're like birch trees, I guess. But short. And their bark is black."

"Felt weird, too," Peter muttered, straightening up, wiping his hands down his coat. "It crumbled when you rubbed it in your hands, like one of those soft block erasers—you know what I mean?"

"We must have stood there ten minutes. More. It was so quiet. You could hear the Sound, although there aren't any waves there or anything. You could hear the big pines behind us dripping. But there weren't any birds. And there wasn't anything moving in that house. Finally, Peter started toward the bell. He took exactly one step into the gazebo, and one of those dwarf trees walked right off its roots into his path, and both of us started screaming."

"What?" said Jenny.

"I didn't scream," said Peter. "And he hit me."

"He barely tapped you," I said.

"He hit me."

"Could you shut up and let Andrew finish?" said Kelly, and Peter lunged, grabbing her slicker in his fists and shoving her hard and then yanking her forward so that her head snapped back like a decapitated flower on its stalk and then snapped into place again.

It had happened so fast that neither Jenny or I moved, but Jenny jumped forward now, raking her nails down Peter's face, and he said, *"Ow!"* and fell back, and she threw her arms around Kelly's shoulders. For a few seconds, they stood like that, and then Kelly put her own arms up and eased Jenny away. To my astonishment, I saw that she was laughing.

"I don't think I'd do that again, if I were you," she said to Peter, her laughter quick and hard, as though she were spitting teeth.

Peter put a hand to his cheek, gazing at the blood that came away on his fingers. "Ow," he said again.

"Let's go home," Jenny said to her sister.

No one answered right away. Then Peter said, "Don't." After a few seconds, when no one reacted, he said, "You've got to see the house." He was going to say more, I think, but what else was there to say? I felt bad without knowing why. He was like a planet we visited, cold and rocky and probably lifeless, and we kept coming because it was all so strange, so different from what we knew. He looked at me, and what I was thinking must have shown in my face, because he blinked in surprise, turned away, and started down the road without looking back. We all followed.

"So the tree hit Peter," Jenny Mack said quietly when we were halfway down the hill, almost to the sheds.

"It wasn't a tree. It just *seemed* like a tree. I don't know how we didn't see him there. He had to have been watching us the whole time. Maybe he knew we'd followed him. He just stepped out of the shadows and kind of poked Peter in the chest with his cane. That black dog-head cane. He did kind of look like a tree. His skin was all gnarly and dark. And his hair was totally white.

"And his voice. It was like a bullfrog. He spoke real slow. He said, 'Boy. Do you know what that bell does?' And then he did the most amazing thing of all. The scariest thing. He looked at both of us, real slow. Then he dropped his cane. Just dropped it to his side. And he smiled, like he was daring us to go ahead. 'That bell raises the dead. Right up out of the ground.'"

"Look at these," Kelly Mack murmured as we walked between the sheds.

"Raises the dead," I said.

"Yeah, I heard you. These are amazing."

And they were. I'd forgotten. The most startling thing, really, was that they were still standing. They'd all sunk into the swampy grass on at least one side, and none of them had roofs, not whole roofs, anyway, and the window slots gaped, and the wind made a rattle as it rolled through them like waves over seashells, empty things that hadn't been empty always. They were too small to have been boat sheds, I thought; they had to have been for tools and things. But tools to do what?

In a matter of steps, they were behind us, between us and the homes we knew, the streets we walked. We reached the ring of pines around the Paars house, and it was different, worse. I didn't realize how, but Peter did.

"No lights," he said.

For a while, we just stood in the blackness while saltwater and pine resin smells glided over us like a mist. There wasn't any moon, but the water beyond the house reflected what light there was, so we could see the long black Lincoln in the dirt driveway, the house and the gazebo beyond it. After a minute or so, we could make out the bell, too, hanging like some bloated white bat from the gazebo ceiling.

"It *is* creepy," Jenny said.

"Ya think?" I said, but I didn't mean to sound the way I did, it was just what I imagined Peter would have said if he were saying anything. "Peter, I think Mr. Paars is gone. Moved, or something."

"Good," he said. "Then he won't mind." He stepped out onto the lawn and said, "Fuck."

"What?" I asked, shoulders hunching, but Peter just shook his head.

"Grass. It's a lot longer. Wet as hell."

"What happened after *'That bell raises the dead'?*" Jenny asked.

I didn't answer right away. I wasn't sure what Peter wanted me to say. But he just squinted at the house and didn't even seem to be listening. I almost took Jenny's hand. I wanted to. "We ran."

"Both of you? Hey, Kell . . ."

But Kelly was already out on the grass next to Peter, smirking as her feet sank. Peter glanced at her, cautiously, I thought. Uncertain. "You would have, too," he said.

"I might have," said Kelly.

Then we were all on the grass, holding still, listening. The wind rushed through the trees as though filling a vacuum. I thought I could hear the Sound. No waves, just the dead, heavy wet. No gulls, no bugs.

Once more, Peter strolled straight for that embedded circle in the grass, still visible despite the depth of the lawn. When Peter's feet crossed the corners of the upside-down triangle—the tear ducts of the eye—I winced, then felt ridiculous. The Macks came with me. I walked in the circle, though I skirted the edge of the triangle. Step on a crack and all. I didn't look behind to see what the Macks did. I was too busy watching Peter as his pace picked up. He was practically running, straight for the gazebo, and then he stopped.

"Hey," he said.

I'd seen it, too, I thought, feeling my knees lock as my nervousness intensified. A flicker in the lone upstairs window. Maybe. Just one, for a single second, and then it was gone again. "I saw it," I called, but Peter wasn't listening to me. He was moving toward the front door. And anyway, I realized, he hadn't been looking upstairs.

"What's he doing?" Kelly said as she strolled past me, but she didn't stop for an answer. Jenny did, though.

"Andrew, what's going on?" she said, and I looked at her eyes, green and shadowy as the grass, but that just made me edgier, still.

I shook my head. For a moment, Jenny stood beside me. Finally, she shrugged and followed her sister. None of them looked back, which meant, I thought, that there really hadn't been rustling behind us just now, back in the pines. When I whipped my head around, I saw nothing but trees and twitching shadows.

"Here, puss-puss-puss," Peter called, meaning me. If the grass had been less wet and I'd been less unsettled, I'd have flopped on my back and flipped my feet in the air at him, the seal's send-off. Instead, I came forward.

The house, like the sheds, seemed to have sunk sideways into the ground. With its filthy windows and rotting planks, it looked like the abandoned hull of a beached ship. Around it, the bent and leafless branches of the dwarf trees waved and flapped in the wind.

"Now, class," said Peter, still very quietly. "What's wrong with this picture?"

"Other than giant bells, weird eyeballs in the grass, empty sheds, and these whammy-ass trees?" Kelly said, but Peter ignored her.

"He means the front door," said Jenny, and of course she was right.

I don't even know how Peter noticed. It was under an over-hang so that the only light that reached it reflected off the ground. But there was no doubt. The door was open. Six inches, tops. The scratched brass of the knob glinted dully like an eye.

"Okay," I said. "So the door didn't catch when he went in, and he didn't notice."

"When *who* went in?" said Peter, mocking. "Thought you said he moved."

The wind kicked up, and the door glided back another few inches, then sucked itself shut with a click.

"Guess that settles that," I said, knowing it didn't even before the curtains came streaming out the single front window, gray and gauzy as cigarette smoke as they floated on the breeze. They hung there a few seconds, then glided to rest against the side of the house when the wind expired.

"Guess it does," Peter said softly, and he marched straight up the steps, pushed open the door, and disappeared into the Paars house.

None of the rest of us moved or spoke. Around us, tree branches tapped against each other and the side of the house. For the second time I sensed someone behind me and spun around. Night dew sparkled in the lawn like broken glass, and one of the shadows of the towering pines seemed to shiver back as though the trees had inhaled it. Otherwise, there was nothing. I thought about Mr. Paars, that dog-head cane with its silver fangs.

"What's he trying to prove?" Kelly asked, a silly question where Peter was concerned, really. It wasn't about proving. We all knew that.

Jenny said, "He's been in there a long time," and Peter stuck his head out the window, the curtain floating away from him.

"Come see this," he said, and ducked back inside.

Hesitating was pointless. We all knew it. We went up the stairs together, and the door drifted open before we even touched it. "Wow," said Kelly staring straight ahead, and Jenny took my hand again, and then we were all inside. "Wow," Kelly said again.

Except for a long, wooden table folded and propped against the staircase like a lifeboat, all the furniture we could see had been draped in white sheets. The sheets rose and rearranged themselves in the breeze, which was constant and everywhere because all the windows had been flung wide open. Leaves chased each other across the dirt-crusted hardwood floor, and scraps of paper flapped in midair like giant moths before settling on the staircase or the backs of chairs or blowing out the windows.

Peter appeared in a doorway across the foyer from us, his black hair bright against the deeper blackness of the rooms behind him. "Don't miss the den," he said. "I'm going to go look at the kitchen." Then he was gone again.

Kelly had started away, now, too, wandering into the living room to our right, running her fingers over the tops of a covered couch as she passed it. One of the paintings on the wall had been covered rather than removed, and I wondered what it was. Kelly drew up the cover, peered beneath it, then dropped it and stepped deeper into the house. I started to follow, but Jenny pulled me the other way, and we went left into what must have been Mr. Paars's den.

"Whoa," Jenny said, and her fingers slid between mine and tightened.

In the dead center of the room, amidst discarded file folders that lay where they'd been tossed and empty envelopes with plastic address-windows that flapped and chattered when the wind filled them, sat an enormous oak rolltop desk. The top was gone, broken away, lying against the room's lone window like the cracked shell of a dinosaur egg. On the surface of the desk in black, felt frames, a set of six photographs had been arranged in a semicircle.

"It's like the top of a tombstone," Jenny murmured. "You know what I mean? Like a . . . what do you call it?"

"Family vault?" I said. "Mausoleum?"

"One of those."

Somehow, the fact that two of the frames turned out to be empty made the array even more unsettling. The other four held individual pictures of what had to be brothers and one sister— they all had flying white hair, icy blue eyes—standing, each in turn, on the top step of the gazebo outside, with the great bell looming behind them, bright white and all out of proportion, like the Mountain on a clear day.

"Andrew," Jenny said, her voice nearly a whisper, and in spite of the faces in the photographs and the room we were in, I felt it all over me. "Why Struwwelpeter?"

"What?" I said, mostly just to make her speak again.

"Struwwelpeter. Why does Mr. Andersz call him that?"

"Oh. It's from some kids' book. My mom actually had it when she was little. She said it was about a boy who got in trouble because he wouldn't cut his hair or his nails."

Jenny narrowed her eyes. "What does that have to do with anything?"

"I don't know. My mom said the pictures in the book were really scary. She said Struwwelpeter looked like Freddy Krueger with a 'fro."

Jenny burst out laughing, but she stopped fast. Neither of us, I think, liked the way laughter sounded in that room, in that house, with those black-bordered faces staring at us. "Struwwelpeter," she said, rolling the name carefully on her tongue, like a little kid who'd been dared to lick a frozen flagpole.

"My mother says Mr. Andersz isn't even saying it right. Can't be, because it's spelled with 'w's' in the middle, and since it's German—"

"It's what my mom called me when I was little," said Peter from the doorway, and Jenny's fingers clenched and fell free of mine. Peter didn't move toward us. He just stood there while we watched, paralyzed. After a few, long seconds, he added, "When I kicked the shit out of barbers, because I hated having my haircut. Then when I was just being bad. She'd say that instead of screaming at me. It made me cry." From across the foyer, in the living room, maybe, we heard a single soft bump, as though something had fallen over.

With a shrug, Peter stepped past us back into the foyer. We

followed, not touching, now, not even looking at each other. I felt guilty, amazed, hollow. When we passed the windows the curtains billowed up and brushed across us.

"Hey, Kelly," Peter whispered loudly, and then, turning our way, he said, "You think he's dead?"

"Looks like it," I answered, glancing down the hallway toward the kitchen, into the shadows in the living room, which seemed to have shifted, somehow, the sheet different in some way as it lay across the couch. I couldn't place the feeling, it was like watching an actor playing a corpse, knowing he was alive, trying to catch him breathing.

"But the car's here," Peter said. "The Lincoln. Hey, *Kelly!*" His shout made me wince, and Jenny cringed back toward the front door, but she shouted, too.

"Kell? *Kell?*"

"Hey. What is *that?*" I murmured, my whole spine twitching like severed electrical wire, and when Jenny and Peter looked at me, I pointed upstairs.

"Wh—" Jenny started, and then it happened again, and both of them saw it. From under the half-closed door at the top of the staircase—the only door we could see from where we were—came a sudden slash of light that disappeared instantly like a snake's tongue flashing in and out.

We stood there at least a minute, maybe more. Even Peter looked uncertain. Not scared, exactly, but something had happened to his face. I couldn't place it, but it made me nervous. And it made me like him more than I had in a long, long time.

Then, without warning, Peter was halfway up the stairs, his feet stomping dust out of each step as he slammed them down, saying, "Fucking hilarious, Kelly. Here I come. Ready or not." He stopped and turned to glare at us. Mostly at me. "Coming?"

"Come on," I said to Jenny, and reached out on my own for the first time and touched her elbow, but to my surprise she jerked it away from me. "Jenny, she's up there."

"I don't think so," she whispered.

"Come *on*," Peter hissed.

"Andrew, something's wrong. Stay here."

I looked into her face, smart, steely Jenny Mack, first girl ever to look at me like that, first girl I'd ever wanted to, and right then, for the only time in my life, I felt within me the horrible thrill of Peter's power, knew the secret of it. It wasn't bravery and it wasn't smarts, although he had both those things in spades. It was simply the willingness to trade. At any given moment, Peter Andersz would trade anyone for anything, or at least could convince people that he would. Knowing you could do that, I thought, would be like holding a grenade with the pin pulled, tossing it back and forth in the terrified face of the world.

I looked at Jenny's eyes, which were filling with tears, and I wanted to kiss her, though I couldn't even imagine how to initiate something like that. What I said, in my best Peter-voice, was, "I'm going upstairs. With or without you."

I can't explain. I didn't mean anything. It felt like playacting, no more real than holding her hand had been. We were just throwing on costumes, dancing around each other, scaring each other. Trick-or-treat.

"*Kelly?*" Jenny called past me, crying openly, now, and I started to reach for her again, and she shoved me, hard, toward the stairs.

"Hurry up," said Peter, with none of the triumph I might have expected in his voice.

I went up, and we clomped, side by side, to the top of the stairs. When we reached the landing, I looked back at Jenny. She was propped in the front door, one hand on the doorknob and the other wiping at her eyes as she jerked her head from side to side, looking for her sister.

At our feet, light licked under the door again. Peter held up a hand, and we stood together and listened. We heard wind, low and hungry, and now I was sure I could hear the Sound lapping against the edge of the continent, crawling over the lip of it.

"Onetwothree*Boo!*" Peter screamed and flung open the door, which banged against a wall inside and bounced back. Peter kicked it open again, and we lunged into what must have been a bedroom, once, and was now just a room, a blank space with nothing in it at all.

Even before the light swept over us again, from outside, from the window, I realized what it was. "Lighthouse," I said, breathless. "Greenpoint Light."

Peter grinned. "Oh, yeah. Halloween."

Every year, the suburbs north of us set Greenpoint Light running again on Halloween, just for fun. One year, they'd even rented ferries and decked them out with seaweed and parents in pirate costumes and floated them just offshore, ghost ships for the kiddies. We'd seen them skirting our suburb on their way up the coast.

"Do you think—" I started, and Peter grabbed me hard by the elbow. "Ow!" I said.

"Listen," snapped Peter.

I heard the house groan as it shifted. I heard paper flapping somewhere downstairs, the front door bumping against its frame or the inside wall as it swung on the wind.

"*Listen,*" Peter whispered, and this time I heard it. Very low. Very faint, like a finger rubbed along the lip of a glass, but unmistakable once you realized what it was. Outside in the yard, someone had lifted the tongue of the bell and tapped it, oh so gently, against the side.

I stared at Peter, and he stared back. Then he leapt to the window, peering down. The way his shoulders jerked, I thought he was going to punch the glass loose.

"Well?" I said.

"All I can see is the roof." He shoved the window even farther open than it already was. *"Clever girls!"* he screamed, and waited, for laughter, maybe, a full-on bong of the bell, something. Abruptly, he turned to me, and the light rolled across him, waist-high, and when it receded, he looked different, damp with it. "Clever girls," he said.

I turned, stepped into the hall, looked down. The front door was open, and Jenny was gone. "Peter?" I whispered, and I heard him swear as he emerged onto the landing beside me. "You think they're outside?"

Peter didn't answer right away. He had his hands jammed in his pockets, his eyes cast down at the floor. He shuffled in place. "The thing is, Andrew, there's nothing to do."

"What are you talking about?"

"There's nothing to do. Here. Anywhere. Now."

"Find the girls?"

He shrugged.

"Ring the bell?"

"They rang it."

"You're the one who brought us out here. What were you expecting?"

He glanced back at the bedroom's bare walls, the rectangular, dustless space in the floor where, until very recently, a bed or rug must have been, the empty light fixture overhead. Struwwelpeter. My friend. "Opposition," he said, and shuffled off down the hall.

"Where are you going?" I called after him.

He glanced back, and the look on his face stunned me. It had been years since I'd seen it. The last time was in second grade, right after he punched Robert Case, who was twice his size, in the face and ground one of Robert's eyeglass lenses into his eye.

The last time anyone who knew him had dared to fight him. He looked . . . sorry.

"This way," he said.

I almost followed him. But I felt bad about leaving Jenny. And I wanted to see her and Kelly out on the lawn, pointing through the window and laughing at us. And I didn't want to stay in that house anymore. And it was exhausting being with Peter, trying to read him, dancing clear of him.

"I'll be outside," I said.

He shrugged and disappeared through the last unopened door at the end of the hall. I listened for a few seconds, heard nothing, and started downstairs. "Hey, Jenny?" I called, but got no answer. I was three steps from the bottom before I realized what was wrong.

In the middle of the foyer floor, amidst a swirl of leaves and paper, Kelly Mack's black baseball cap lay upside down like an empty tortoise shell. "Um," I said to no one, to myself. I took one more uncertain step, and the front door swung back on its hinges.

I just stared, at first. I couldn't even breathe, it was as if I had an apple core lodged in my throat. I just stared into the white spray paint on the front door, the triangle within a circle. A wet, wide open eye. My legs wobbled, and I grabbed for the banister, slipped down to the bottom step, held myself still. I should scream, I thought. I should get Peter down here, and both of us should run. I didn't see the hand until it clamped hard around my mouth.

For a second, I couldn't do anything at all, and that was way too long, because before I could lurch away or bite down, a second hand snaked around my waist and I was yanked off my feet into the blackness to my left and slammed against the living room wall.

I wasn't sure when I'd closed my eyes, but now I couldn't make them open. My head rang, and my skin felt tingly, tickly, as though it was dissolving into the atoms that made it up, all of them racing in a billion different directions, and soon there'd be nothing left of me, just a scatter of energy and a spot on Mr. Paars's dusty, decaying floor.

"Did I hurt you?" whispered a voice I knew, close to my ears. It still took me a long time to open my eyes. "Just nod or shake your head."

Slowly, forcing my eyes open, I shook my head.

"Good. Now sssh," said Mr. Andersz, and released me.

Behind him, both Mack sisters stood grinning.

"You like the cap on the floor?" Kelly said. "The cap's a good touch, no?"

"Sssh," Mr. Andersz said. "Please. I beg you."

"You should see you," Jenny whispered, sliding up close. "You look so scared."

"What's—"

"He followed us to see if we were doing anything horrible. He saw us come in here, and he had this idea to get back at Peter."

I gaped at Jenny, then Mr. Andersz, who was peering very carefully around the corner, up the stairs.

"Not to get back," he said, and he sounded so serious. It was the same voice he'd used in his own front hallway earlier that evening. He'd never looked more like his son than he did at that moment. "To reach out. Reach him. Someone's got to do something. He's a good boy. He could be. Now, please. Don't spoil this."

Everything about Mr. Andersz's being here astounded me. But watching him revealed nothing further. He stood at the edge of the living room, shoulders hunched, hair tucked tight under his dockworker's cap, waiting. Slowly, my gaze swung back to Jenny, who continued to grin in my direction but not at me, certainly not with me. And I knew I'd lost her.

"This was about Peter," I said. "You could have just stuck your head out and waved me down."

"Yep," said Jenny, and watched Mr. Andersz, not me.

Upstairs, a door creaked, and Peter's voice rang out. "Hey, Andrew."

To Jenny's surprise and Mr. Andersz's horror, I almost answered. I stepped forward, opened my mouth. I'm sure Jenny thought I was trying to get back at her, turn the tables again, but mostly, I didn't like what Mr. Andersz was doing. I think I sensed the danger in it. I might have been the only one.

But I was twelve. And Peter certainly deserved it. And Mr. Andersz was my teacher, and my friend's father. I closed my mouth, sank back into the shadows, and did not move again until it was over.

"Andrew, I know you can hear me!" Peter shouted, stepping onto the landing. He came, clomp-clomp-clomp, toward the stairs. *"Annn-drew!"* Then, abruptly, we heard him laugh. Down he came, his shoes clattering over the steps. I thought he might charge past us, but he stopped right where I did.

Beside the couch, under the draped painting, Kelly Mack pointed at her own hatless head and mouthed, *"Oh, yeah."*

But it was the eye on the door, I thought, not the cap. Only the eye would have stopped him, because like me—and faster than me—Peter would have realized that neither Mack sister, smart as they were, would have thought of it, or even known about the eye before we came here. Even if they'd brought spray paint. Mr. Andersz had brought spray paint? Clearly, he'd been planning this—or something like this—for quite some time. If he was the one who'd done it, that is.

"What the fuck," Peter muttered. He came down a step.

Another. His feet touched flat floor, and still Mr. Andersz held his post.

Then, very quietly, he said, "Boo."

It was as if he'd punched an ejector-seat button. Peter flew through the front door, hands flung up to ward off the eye as he sailed past it. He was fifteen feet from the house, in a dead sprint, when he realized what he'd heard. We all saw it hit him. He jerked like a hooked marlin reaching the end of a harpoon rope.

For a few seconds, he stood in the wet grass with his back to us, quivering. Kelly had sauntered past Mr. Andersz onto the front porch, laughing. Mr. Andersz, I noticed, was smiling too, weakly. Even Jenny was laughing quietly beside me.

But I was watching Peter's back, his whole body vibrating like an imploded building after the charge has gone off, right at the moment of collapse. "No," I said.

When Peter finally turned around, though, his face was his regular face, inscrutable, a little pale. The spikes in his hair looked almost silly in the shadows, and made him look younger. A naughty little boy. Calvin with no Hobbes.

"So he *is* dead," Peter said.

Mr. Andersz stepped outside. Kelly was slapping her leg, but no one paid her any attention.

"Son." Mr. Andersz stretched one hand out, as though to call Peter to him. "I'm sorry. It was . . . I thought you might laugh."

"He's dead, right?"

The smile was gone from Mr. Andersz's face now, and from Jenny's, I noted when I glanced her way. "Kelly, shut up," I heard her say to her sister, and Kelly stopped giggling.

"Did you know he used to teach at the school?" Mr. Andersz asked, startling me.

"Mr. Paars?"

"Sixth-grade science. Biology, especially. Years ago. Kids didn't like him. Yes, Peter, he died a week or so ago. He'd been very sick. We got a notice about it at school."

"Then he won't mind," said Peter, too quietly, "if I go ahead and ring that bell. Right?"

Mr. Andersz didn't know about the bell, I realized. He didn't understand. I watched him look at his son, watched the weight he always seemed to be carrying settle back around his shoulders, lock into place like a yoke. He bent forward, a little.

"My son," he said. Uselessly.

So I shoved past him. I didn't mean to push him, I just needed him out of the way, and anyway, he gave no resistance, bent back like a plant.

"Peter, don't do it," I said.

The eyes, black and mesmerizing, swung down on me. "Oh. Andrew. Forgot you were here."

It was, of course, the cruelest thing he could have said, the source of his power over me and the reason I was with him. Other than the fact that I liked him, I mean. It was the thing I feared most, in general, no matter where I was.

"That bell . . ." I said, thinking of the dog's-head cane, that deep and frozen voice, but thinking more, somehow, about my friend, rocketing away from us now at incomprehensible speed. Because that's what he seemed to be doing, to me.

"Wouldn't it be great?" said Peter. And then, unexpectedly, he grinned at me. He would never forget I was there, I realized. Couldn't. I was all he had.

He walked off across the grass. The Mack sisters and Mr. Andersz followed, all of them seeming to float in the long, wet green like seabirds skimming the surface of the ocean. I did not go with them. I had the feel of Jenny's fingers in mine, and the sounds of flapping paper and whirling leaves in my ears, and Peter's last, surprising smile floating in front of my eyes, and it was enough, too much, an astonishing Halloween.

"This thing's freezing," I heard Peter say, while his father and the Macks fanned out around him, facing the house and me. He was facing away, toward the trees. "Feel this." He held the tongue of the bell toward Kelly Mack, but she'd gone silent now, and she shook her head.

"Ready or not," he said. Then he reared back and rammed the bell tongue home.

Instinctively, I flung my hands up to my ears, but the effect was disappointing, particularly to Peter. It sounded like a dinner bell, high, a little tinny, something that might call kids or a dog out of the water or the woods at dinnertime. Peter slammed the tongue against the side of the bell one more time, dropped it, and the peal floated away over the Sound, dissipating into the salt air like a seagull cry.

For a few breaths, barely any time at all, we all stood where we were. Then Jenny Mack said, "Oh." I saw her hand snake out, grab her sister's, and her sister looked up, right at me, I thought. The two Macks stared at each other. Then they were gone, hurtling across the yard, straight across that wide open white eye, flying toward the forest.

Peter looked at me, and his mouth pursed a little. I couldn't hear him, but I saw him murmur, "Wow," and a new smile exploded, one I couldn't even fathom, and he was gone, too, sprinting for the trees, passing the Macks as they all vanished into the shadows.

"Uh," said Mr. Andersz, backing, backing, and his expression confused me most of all. He was almost laughing. "I'm so sorry," he said. "We didn't realize . . ." He turned and chased after his son. And still, somehow, I thought they'd all been looking at me, until I heard the single sharp thud from the porch behind me. Wood hitting wood. Cane-into-wood.

I didn't turn around. Not then. What for? I knew what was behind me. Even so, I couldn't get my legs to move, quite, not until I heard a second thud, closer this time, as though the thing on the porch had stepped fully out of the house, making its slow, steady way toward me. Stumbling, I kicked myself forward, put a hand down in the wet grass and the mud closed over it like a mouth. When I jerked it free, it made a disappointed, sucking sort of sound, and I heard a sigh behind me, another thud, and I ran all the way to the woods.

Hours later, we were still huddled together in the Anderszs' kitchen, wolfing down Ho Hos and hot chocolate. Jenny and Kelly and Peter kept erupting into cloudbursts of laughter and excited conversation. Mr. Andersz laughed, too, as he boiled more water and spooned marshmallows into our mugs and told us.

The man the bell had called forth, he said, was Mr. Paars's brother. He'd been coming for years, taking care of Mr. Paars after he got too sick to look after himself, because he refused to move into a rest home or even his brother's home.

"The Lincoln," Peter said, and Mr. Andersz nodded.

"God, poor man. He must have been inside when you all got there. He must have thought you were coming to rob the place, or vandalize it, and he went out back."

"We must have scared the living shit out of him," Peter said happily.

"Almost as much as we did you," said Kelly, and all of them were shouting, pointing, laughing again.

"Mr. Paars had been dead for days when they found him," Mr. Andersz told us. "The brother had to go away, and he left a nurse in charge. But the nurse got sick, I guess, or Mr. Paars wouldn't let her in, or something. Anyway, it was pretty awful when the brother came back. That's why the windows were open. It'll take weeks, I bet, to air that place out."

I sat, and I sipped my cocoa, and I watched my friends chatter and eat and laugh and wave their arms around, and it dawned on me, slowly, that none of them had seen. None of them had heard. Not really. I almost said something five different times, but I never quite did, I think because of the way we all were, just for that hour, that last, magic night: giddy and windswept and defiant and together. Like real friends. Almost.

That was the last time, of course. The next summer, the Macks moved to Vancouver, although they'd slowly slipped away from Peter and me anyway by then. Mr. Andersz lost his job— there was an incident, he just stopped teaching one day and sat down on the floor in the front of his classroom and swallowed an entire box of chalk, stick by stick—and wound up working in the little caged accounting office at the used-car lot in the wasteland down by the Ballard Bridge. And slowly, over the next few years, it became more exciting, even for me, to talk about Peter than it was to be with him.

Soon, I think, my mother is going to get sick of staring at the images repeating over and over on our TV screen, the live reports from the rubble of our school and last year's yearbook photo of Peter and the video of him being stuffed into a police car and the names streaming across the bottom of the screen like a tornado warning except too late. For the fifteenth time, at least, I see Steve Rourke's name go by. I should have told him, I thought, should have warned him. But he should have known. I wonder why my name isn't up there, why Peter didn't come after me. The answer, though, is obvious. He forgot I was there. Or he wants me to think he did.

It doesn't matter. Any minute, my mother's going to get up and go to bed, and she's going to tell me I should, too, and that we'll leave here, we'll get away and never come back.

"Yes," I'll say. "Soon."

"All those children," she'll say. Again. "Sweet Jesus, I can't believe it, Andrew." She'll drop her head on my shoulder and throw her arms around me and cry.

But by then, I won't be thinking about the streaming names, the people I knew who are people no longer, or what finally triggered Peter into action tonight. I'll be thinking, just as I am now, about Peter in the grass outside the Paars house, at the moment he realized what we'd done to him. The way he stood there vibrating.

We didn't make him what he was. Not the Macks, not his dad, not me—none of us. But now there's only one thing left to do. As soon as my mom finally lets go, stops sobbing, and stumbles off to sleep, I'm going to sneak outside, and I'm going to go straight down the hill to the Paars house. I haven't been there since that night. I have no idea if the sheds or the house or the bell even exist, anymore.

But if they do, and if that eye in the grass, or any of its power, is still there . . . well, then. I'll give a little ring. And then we'll know, once and for all, whether I really did see *two* old men with matching canes on the porch of the Paars house when I glanced back, right as I fled into the woods. Whether I really did hear rustling from all those sideways sheds as I flew past, as though, in each, something was sliding out of the ground. I wonder if the bell works only on the Paars family, or if it affects any recently deceased in the vicinity. Maybe the dead really can be called back, for a while, like kids from recess. And if they do come back—and if they're angry, and they go looking for Peter, and they find him—well. Let the poor, brilliant, fucked-up bastard get what he deserves.

Shipwreck Beach

"According to mystical people, spiritual forces converge at Hawai'i, as do ocean currents and winds."

—MAXINE HONG KINGSTON,
HAWAI'I ONE SUMMER

They served us guava punch and Paradise Mix, which turned out to be candied peanuts, coconut flakes, and dried papaya, and far below, in the long expanses between islands, the water glowed green and blue, too wet, somehow, like the insides of some luscious, cracked-open tropical fruit. I couldn't get the light out of my eyes even when I shut them. Across the narrow aisle from me, the woman with the laptop snapped her computer shut as we landed, looked up for the first time since takeoff, and said, "God, can you feel that air?"

The exit door wasn't even open, and something about the intensity in her voice made me snort.

The woman whirled as though I'd shot a rubber band at her. She had green eyes—ordinary, mainland green—and skeletal protruding shoulders under her white silk blouse.

"Well?" she said. "Can't you?"

And I realized that I could. The feeling came in with the light. I blushed, and the door up front opened, and the woman sheathed her laptop and strode out. The lone flight attendant stepped back practically into the cockpit when she passed, waited for the other seven passengers to deplane, then stood there, not quite looking at my legs in the aisle, waiting. Self-conscious, as usual—not to mention tanless—I tugged the hem of my skirt down over my knees. He looked a little older than I was, maybe twenty, his skin rich and dark and rough. He had black hair and big hands. He shifted, aimed his gaze a little closer to my eyes, and said, "Aloha, and welcome to Lana-ii." The hiccup in the name sounded like something he'd practiced, not natural to him.

"Okay," I said, because I'd wanted to come, after all. Demanded to come. Pleaded, until my mother had finally broken down and let me, because Harry had begged me. And now here I was. Damn him.

God, I remember that moment, stepping onto Lanai for the first time, blinking against the sunlight and feeling the trade winds tumble past. I squinted, eyeing the square, squat, wooden terminal and the single luggage cart trundling out to meet the plane as passengers spilled onto the tarmac. Around us, low green hills swelled and sank. Petrified waves, I thought. That's all this place was. The last land. The farthest Harry could run. I shouldered my duffel bag, took two steps toward the terminal and saw him.

He'd lost so much weight that he seemed to have shed his shadow, and his skin was dark, as if he'd been out of jail for ten years, not ten months. But he still wore the same, stupid glasses, brown-tinted and curvy, so that his eyes seemed to bulge behind them like a lizard's. When he spotted me, he bounced up and down on the balls of his feet, and I half-expected him to jump the restraining rope set up for nonpassengers.

Instead, he waited until I was inside the rope, standing next to him, starting to say something salty, and then he engulfed me.

"Get off," I mumbled after a few seconds, because amazingly, he smelled even worse than I remembered. Ammonia, now, and citronella, and pineapple, on top of the mentholated shaving cream and hair gel and drugstore cologne.

"Hello, cousin," he said, not even loosening his grip, and I snapped my elbows out, grabbed his wrists, shoved him up onto his tiptoes and jammed my foot against the ball of his ankle.

"Could've broken that," I said.

"You really are fast."

I let go of his wrists, stepped back before he could hug me again, and put my hands together. "Hai."

"Hi, Mimi," Harry said.

"Not hi, idiot. *Hai*, as in yes, I really am fast." I bowed. "Ous."

Somehow, he'd scooped his haystack of blond hair into a

poofy Bill Clinton–wave. Despite the weight loss, he looked soft in his button-down Hawaiian shirt, complete with embroidered palm trees. Of my cousin the swimmer, the boy who, barely ten years ago, had shattered the Orange County fourteen-and-under record in the 200 fly, there was little trace.

"Well, let's go see it," I said, and Harry blinked.

"See what?"

"The beach with the ghost wreck. The one you keep e-mailing me about."

"We can't just go see that. It has to be right."

"Let's see now."

"Later."

"What, you want to show me the multiplex?" I gestured around me at the empty green. "The jammin' club scene?"

"Thank you, Mimi," Harry whispered, and wetness formed in the corners of his lizard eyes under his glasses. "Thank you for coming."

I watched until the tears leaked onto his cheek. Then I blurted, "Fuck my mother," spun on my heels, and started through the terminal. I heard Harry galumphing behind me, graceless as a hippo, mumbling something about not talking about her like that, but I didn't turn around. In my ears, I could hear my mother recounting, for the thousandth time, the story of the day Harry's parents put him on the train from OC and sent him down to visit us in Solana Beach. This was before the incident with the necklace, before he got thrown out of school for selling or maybe just being near selling, before the car-jacking-and-burning thing, any of it, when all eleven-year-old Harry had done was fake results on a biology project about the effects of Jodie Foster's Army music on plant growth, earn a series of report-card comments about his "elusiveness when confronted," and throw a bicycle pump through his teacher's car's back window, which he swore was an accident. That last had just occurred, though no one had told me about it, and was the reason my aunt had shipped him off to us for the weekend so she and my uncle could calm down, "get our heads straight."

I was six, and I remember standing at the Del Mar train station, which was mostly a shack and looked exactly like the shacks across the street from it on the lip of the beach, where you could rent boogie boards and buy waffle cones with chocolate syrup colored blue, just because. I'd already been in the water, I think, because I remember the slick of salt on my skin, the faint sting in my eyes every time I blinked, the skateboard boys floating past, white-shirted, wild-haired.

Then the train came whistling and growling into the station and sighed to a stop, and I remember how huge it seemed, huff, puff, blow your house down. Seconds later, Harry charged out, sprinting straight for us with his legs pumping under his tan OP's and his green surf shirt billowing around him. He threw himself straight into my mother's arms. That's what I remember. I don't remember him saying, "God, Aunt Trish, I love you so incredibly much, you look beautiful," which is what my mother damns him for, but I'm sure he did. Those are the kinds of things he said.

"I knew right then," my mother would say, from that moment on, every time her sister called weeping, recounting Harry's latest inexplicable, increasingly unforgivable act. "You could just tell. It was too much, you know? Off, somehow. Calculated. You just knew that boy would say absolutely anything to anybody. Do absolutely anything to get what he wanted." What made me so furious, every time, was the nagging, inescapable possibility that she was right.

Exiting the terminal, I turned on Harry and snapped, "Where's the bus? Or are we walking?"

He was closer behind than I'd expected, and he cocked his head when he stopped, peering at me from under his bulgy lenses. Turtle-cousin. "Come on, Harry," I said, and was relieved to hear my voice sound gentler this time. "Show me the isle."

For a few seconds, he just stood there swaying, which fanned my annoyance again. Once upon a time, Harry had been the only person immune to my mood swings, which my mother had dubbed the Tradewinds of Amelia long before Harry moved here. My mother said they didn't affect Harry because Harry was oblivious to anyone but himself.

Finally, for the first time since I'd stepped off the plane, my cousin grinned. "I have a car." The grin twitched.

I grinned back, partly to encourage him, partly because it was either that or kick him. "How'd that happen?"

"Work. I teach at the grade school. They fronted me some money to get me started."

Now it was my turn to stare. "Teach what?"

He shrugged. "They don't check backgrounds so much out here. It's a new chance, you know? A real one."

From his pants pocket, he withdrew a set of keys, pressed a button, got an answering squawk from a green Toyota pickup so sparkly-clean it seemed to ripple like the surface of the sea, and beamed the way he used to, bobbing in the surf, when the big waves rose and swept him up. I slung my bag in the bed.

As soon as we were out of the parking lot, the island opened beneath us like a gorgeous green flipped-over umbrella drifting on the winking water. I saw pineapple plants sticking out of the ground in rows, their spiky fruits nestled in the long, straight leaves like nesting birds.

In front of us, a salt-caked blue bus filled the road, headed our way. Harry pulled to the side into the dirt, and when the driver passed—another Hawaiian boy, no older than the flight attendant on my plane, with a white cap that read *Manele Bay* in red letters perched on his forehead—he stuck his hand out the window, palm down, and waved. Harry waved back, same way, and something quivered in my chest. Aunt Fred should come here, I thought. See this.

"I want to see your school," I said.

Harry held onto the wheel and glanced at me. "You in shape? Swim-shape, I mean?"

I flicked the jiggly pouch of flesh under his bicep. "More than you."

Harry blushed. "Did you dye your hair?"

"Do you remember it red? Is that like a question?"

"It looks nice," he mumbled, straight down into the steering wheel, and I felt bad, and we were off again.

For a while, we drove without talking. Harry rolled his window down, so I did, too, and the smell came in: sea salt and wet grass and most of all, gardenia, so sweet, too much, as though a perfume factory had exploded nearby. Lanai air, it turns out, is as addicting as cigarette smoke. You forget how to breathe without smelling.

We passed another bus, a few road signs rusting and tilting in the ocean wind, white condominiums jutting from the hillsides like false teeth. Finally, Harry pulled to a stop along a curve in the road and shut down the truck and got out. I started to do the same, and he leaned back in.

"Change," he said.

It took me a second to realize what he meant. Then I said, "Here?"

"I'll be up the hill." He gestured to the green rise beside the car.

"Is this the wreck?"

"I told you," he said, straightening, so that his voice got all but swallowed by the wind. "I want to share that with you the right way. I want you to feel it, too. That way, you might understand."

"Is this a religion thing? Did you get Jesus or something?"

With a shrug, Harry swung the door shut and grabbed twin sets of flippers and masks out of the truck bed and started up the hill. Beneath the white canvas shorts, his leg muscles tensed and slackened like cleated rope on mastheads. The softness, I thought, had not spread there. And he really did seem closer to peaceful than I'd ever seen him, if no less sad. In the visiting room at California State Prison in Lancaster, both times my mother let me go, he'd dissolved into a blubbering, whimpering mess across the table and managed to say virtually nothing. Clearly, the island or the sun or his holy shipwreck had done something for him. To him.

I had to get out of the car and drag the duffel bag into the dirt so I could unzip it, then crouch back inside the cab to wriggle into my suit. As usual, my legs looked stumpy to me. Neither karate nor swimming had lengthened them any. "But the hair," I said aloud, catching sight of myself in the mirror on the sun visor, "is red."

I was expecting ocean at my feet, white sand smooth as a glacier but hot, fanning away in all directions. What I found when I got to the top of the hill was ocean, alright, but sixty feet or so below, slamming so hard against the rock face we stood on that I could feel the vibrations in my feet. Eyeing Harry, I said, "Is this a test?"

He shook his head. "More of a warm-up."

"Physical? Spiritual?" I was teasing as much as asking.

Harry slid his hands into his pockets and stepped onto the foot-wide path that slanted down the rocks. There was no beach below, but Harry didn't even slow as he reached the lowest exposed point on the path, just dropped his shirt and my flippers to the dirt and slid his own fins onto his feet and plunged into the surf. I hustled after him, stopping only long enough to check for coral or rock before I leapt. The peaks in the water looked more like rumples in a thrashed-about sheet than waves because they had no whitecaps and they didn't break except when they slammed against the cliff.

Then the ocean had me, and I thought about nothing but breathing. I didn't even look up for the first three minutes, just drove forward. My mouth stung with salt water, and my legs kept pounding as I plunged from wave trough to wave trough. Competing currents twisted around my ankles below the surface, grabbed, released. Glancing up finally, I saw our destination, the pillar of crooked brown rock sticking out of the surf like a giant's beckoning finger, seemingly no closer than it had been when I leapt from the ledge.

When I felt I was free of the caldron near shore, at least, I looked up again, spit, and called after my cousin. "Not really supposed to swim here, are we?"

Far ahead, Harry glided to a stop, rolled over on his back, and cupped a hand to his ear. As always, he'd lost all his awkwardness as soon as he hit the water, become sleek and slippery and playful as an otter.

"Swim here," I yelled again, kicking hard, lurching toward him as he hovered in place. "Supposed to?"

"Not much 'supposed to' on Lanai," he said. "No one checking."

"But people don't. Swim here."

Harry grinned. "You *are* rusty." Then he flipped over again, shot ahead of me, and I followed as best I could.

For the next ten minutes or so, I did what he'd trained me to do years ago as he skated across the insides of waves or scaled them like a mountain climber, seeming, sometimes, to emerge, fully standing, atop them as they curled, as if he were about to plant a flag there: I put my head down, looked neither forward nor back, and kicked steadily while my nerve ends read the water. Sometimes I tacked against the current, and sometimes I ran before it, cupping it in my ribs it the way a sail grabs wind. When I let myself look up again, the rock was close enough for me to see that there was nowhere to grab, no place to rest. Solid sheets of perfect green water shattered against it like china plates.

"You okay?" Harry said, surfacing beside me, pulling up short, bobbing. So I pulled up, too, nodded, and found, to my relief, that I was. My shoulders were screaming, and my thigh muscles filled my skin like poured concrete, hardening, but the air was flying down my lungs into my bloodstream, lighting me up as it went, and I could feel myself tingling, awakening. Not even karate made me feel quite this strong.

"That's nowhere we can go," I said, and Harry nodded.

"It's somewhere to see. There's a story. Want to hear it?"

Abruptly, I swung toward him. There was a story I wanted to hear, okay—needed to hear—but it wasn't the one Harry wanted to tell me. So I just up and asked him. "How did it happen, Harry? Please make me understand."

"The rock? It—"

"Randy Lynne, Harry. Prison, Harry. How did that happen? What the fuck is wrong with you?"

He buckled as though a wave had slammed him, ducked under water, and for a second, I thought he'd left me there, dove for his lair or whatever he'd apparently built for himself here. But he surfaced again. Bobbing. Effortless.

"I'm sorry," I said. "I've tried. But I can't seem to make myself understand."

"Me either," Harry said softly, staring at the rock and the empty sea beyond it.

"Was it bad? Prison?" As soon as I asked that, I felt like an idiot. And I knew what he was going to say.

"It's where I belonged," he murmured, right on cue. Then he went quiet, absolutely still, as though he was going to let himself sink.

"Harry," I said quickly. "Listen. You're a fucking idiot, right? I agree with you. But get real. You did what everyone does. Lots of people, anyway. You just got caught."

Harry's head shot up so fast I thought he'd been stung or bitten, and I started to kick toward him and then checked myself, hard. In his stare, and in the set of his lips, chewed to shreds the way they always were, was something brand new. It looked, I thought, like loathing.

"The man died," he said.

I found I couldn't look at him. I looked at the rock. "You weren't even driving. You—"

"Shut up, Mimi. Right now."

More than anything, I needed to get his glare off me. I could feel it on my arms and face like radiation. "Tell me about the rock," I said, remembering Harry, age fifteen or so, skimming the waves off Laguna Niguel like a gull.

"Pu'upehe," Harry said. I have no idea if he said the word right, but he sounded more Hawaiian to my distinctly haole ears than the flight attendant or pilot on my plane. "There's a story. A girl. So beautiful, her husband shut her up in a sea cave." He gestured behind us toward the cliffs, but he didn't look that way. His voice came out raspy, as though I'd kicked him in the throat.

"I'm sorry, Harry," I said. "I just missed you, and I don't—"

"One day when the husband was out hunting or something, a storm came, and the sea swirled in, filled the cave, and the woman drowned there. When the husband came back and found her, he was so overwhelmed with grief that he dragged his wife's body into the sea, somehow swam with it to this rock, hauled it up to the top, and buried it there. Then he jumped into the water and drowned."

Harry looked at me, too hard, his blond hair flying off his head like steam, and a new nervousness spasmed through me. Another gift from my mother, I realized. She'd always thought it just might be a little wrong, the way Harry loved me.

"Mimi, look down," he said suddenly, and drove his head below the surface.

At first, when I dropped my face in the water, I couldn't make sense of it. There were so many of them, fanned out in perfect rows, that they looked more like the long leaves of some underwater kelp forest than individual creatures. Then four of them broke from the line, swept upward at us, and whirled around us, their bodies steel-green, so smooth I swear I could see my reflection sliding across them, their chitter and squeak filling the water like bat sonar. One of them hurtled clear of the surface, and I jerked my head up in time to see it finish its flip and crash down not five feet from me, and I burst out laughing as spray smacked into my mouth, rocking me backward. Coughing, still laughing, I ducked under again, found another one hovering right in front of me, snout all but touching my chest, mouth open so I could see the startling teeth, the tiny black eyes swallowing sunlight but radiating nothing like slivers of coal. It looked utterly alien up close in its world, nothing at all like me, and yet never, ever, ever had I been more aware of the sizzle in the skin, the ripple in the blood that tells you another living thing is near.

Fifteen seconds, maybe twenty, and it was over. The whole school swung like a hinged gate toward the open ocean, and in a matter of seconds they were a hundred yards away, leaping clear of the water and crashing back and finally disappearing altogether, leaving barely a wisp of white on the white-capped water to show where they had been.

"Oh my God, Harry!" I sputtered, gagging and giggling.

"Come on." He looked away from me now. "You'll get tired." He kicked toward shore, but I caught a glimpse of his face as he dropped it into the water. His smile must have lit the reef.

Back in the truck, and then at the restaurant at the Manele Bay Hotel, Harry barely spoke, wouldn't even let me catch his eye, so I just sat and surrounded myself with the dolphins of Pu'upehe, the light in all that silvered skin and that clamorous, squeaking chatter. But finally, inevitably, another voice rose in their midst and scattered them like killer-whale shriek. My mother's, of course, recounting, yet again, exactly what Harry had done.

First, apparently, he'd bought two cases of Red Hook for Randy Lynne and his goofy little band of goons. Harry was still something of a legend for Randy and the rest of the next-gen thugs at my school; they sought him out sometimes at the TruSavings Hardware where he worked in the stockroom and made him tell them the car-burning story. They were almost too funny and too smart to be thugs, those boys. Almost. What they liked to do, mostly, was snort glue—not even smoke pot—and then go to the mall and mess up stores. Rearrange the science-fiction section in reverse-alphabetical order at the Walden books, or switch the price tags at the Williams-Sonoma. They reminded Harry of Harry, I think, although they were funnier, and more clever, and more smug. Anyway, he told me once, if they were wasting time talking to him, they weren't bothering anyone else.

None of which explains why, on the night he bought them Red Hook, he took them out riding, and let Randy drive, after watching Randy chug nine of the beers by himself. Somehow, they wound up at the S-curves down past the Orange Grove Mall, where the tract homes sink into the desert-bare hillsides and coyotes slink along the roadbeds, prowling for car-struck cats and rabbits. There weren't any other vehicles in sight, so Harry let Randy perch them at the top of the rise, then floor the gas and send them plummeting through the curves while his goons screamed "I'm a Little Bit Country, She's a Little Bit Rock-and-Roll" in the crammed backseat. What they hit, Harry told the cops later, barely made a sound, didn't even seem like anything solid. It just snapped under the tires and shot out the back like a paper bag. Harry had jammed his feet on top of Randy's, sending the car screeching into a u-turn and very nearly flipping them over as Randy screamed, "The *fuck*, man?"

Then they all saw it. After that, Harry says they sat there for a really long time.

Of course, Randy announced, "We gotta leave. We gotta go now."

So Harry punched him in the face, hard enough to split both his lips against his teeth, and got out of the car. He told me—later, in jail—that even with the man lying splayed that way, even with the gurgle Harry was just beginning to realize he could hear, he had this momentary but overwhelming sensation that everything was alright. A trick of the canyon, cradling the warm evening air and the moonlight like a cupped palm.

But the gurgle turned out to be wind in flattened lungs, and there was a shushing, too, the sound of blood sluicing across the pavement as though squirted from a sprinkler. When Harry was almost on top of him, the man's arm shot up like a wing, as though he was about to take flight. Then, somehow, the man screwed his head around—like an owl, Harry said, it was practically all the way backward—and opened his eyes wide. Blood kept rushing into the horrible, indented places in his body like water into footprints and filling them.

"I'm so sorry," Harry said, stumbling to his knees.

"*Puto*," the man whispered, somehow. Then he died.

During the first few months of his jail term, Harry wrote letter after letter to newspapers, the INS, the business offices of the corporations that run the flower fields and the last of Orange County's orange groves. But no one ever determined who the dead man was.

"An alien," one of the guards assured Harry one night, when he couldn't sleep and wound up sitting against the door of his cell, tapping the bars quietly with a toothpick. "Bet on it."

According to Harry, that comment was supposed to be comforting. *Alien,* as in stray dog, possum. But it just made my cousin feel worse. From then on, he dreamed—when he slept, which wasn't often—of twin girls in flower-print dresses leaning flyers against the cardboard walls of shacks in migrant camps, setting them against highway signs because the girls had no tape to affix them, holding them to the air so they scattered like milkweed. The flyers had no photographs on them, no face. Just the two words. *PADRE.* And *MISSING,* because whatever the Spanish was for that, Harry didn't know it.

2

After dinner, Harry took me wandering on the hotel grounds, and we wound up ordering mango sundaes and eating them by the pool. The water looked completely orange in the fading light, as though the sun had melted into it, and down the hill, through the trees, I could see ocean, and my skin buzzed with the memory of the dolphins, and it seemed I could feel all the impossible life surrounding and overrunning this place through my feet, sweeping up from the ground like electrical current. In one of the perfectly landscaped tropical glades around us, a luau had started, and I could smell meat roasting and hear swaying guitars and voices singing that Buddy Holly song, "Oh Boy," like it was tribal chant, an ode to husbands and brothers lost to the sea.

"Harry," I said, pushing my bowl back and licking the orange syrup from my lips, "you have never shown me a better day." I watched him stare down at his plate, grip his napkin in his fist like a cross and then release it. "No one has. I hate my mother."

"You do not," Harry murmured. "I certainly don't."

"She hates you," I snapped, because I couldn't bear the sticky softness in his voice, and because it was true, and he needed to know it. My mother wasn't ever going to forgive him.

Harry winced, then looked at me. There were tears in his eyes, but the wrong kind. The grateful kind again. "She still trusts me enough to send you here."

"She trusts *me*, you moron," I said, threw my napkin down, and stalked past the lounge chairs, out to the top of the hill over-looking the beach. The second the sun had gone, the full moon floated up the sky, a giant halo ringing it like the flickering, translucent bell of a jellyfish. It will never be dark here, I was thinking. There's too much light.

After a while—a respectful few minutes—Harry took his place at my elbow, careful not to graze me, and we watched the moon on the water. Then he said, "Want to play pool?"

"You have a pool table?"

"The hotel does."

"We're not guests of the hotel."

"They don't mind," Harry said. "It's not like there's lots of other places for the locals to go."

He led me back past the pool, the little kids still splashing on kickboards in the shallow end and the old people lounging in the hot tub with their umbrella drinks arrayed around them, past one of the circular stone ponds where giant red and black goldfish clung to the bottom with their scales glinting metallic in the moonlight and their eyes enormous, fairy-tale creatures made of wishing-well pennies. We climbed a palatial white staircase, trailing salt air and ukulele strum, and reentered the lounge, where guests sat scattered among the overstuffed chairs and throw pillows, playing hearts or reading paperbacks. Everywhere, there were feet half out of flip-flops, heads nestled deep in pillows, little white dessert plates streaked with veins of raspberry sauce, chocolate syrup, and melted ice cream, like summer-camp crafts projects awaiting the kiln. Through it all strolled my cousin, nodding at no one but knowing where he was going, hands in the pockets of his baggy white beach shorts, swim-strong legs pumping him forward. He didn't look native, just home, which was more than enough to make me want to weep.

Down outdoor corridors Harry led me, past rooms with their doors thrown open to the evening, past the concierge's bungalow, where he nodded at a Hawaiian woman in a sleek gray business suit saying something about tee times into her headset phone, and, finally, into Puhi's Den.

Despite the wisps of cigarette smoke disintegrating in the air and the Biz Markie song bumping from the speakers and shaking the floor, Puhi's felt more like a playroom than a bar. Where the windows should have been was wide-open space framed by thatch from the surrounding palms, which made the whole place look like a tree house. On every tabletop, citronella candles licked at their cylindrical glass casings with long orange tongues. From a round hole cut into the wall above the door frame, the head of a giant papier-mâché eel loomed, mouth gaping in that moray way that looks so much like bite-about-to-happen and is really just breathing.

"Fried plantains?" Harry said, surprising me with his smile.

"Pineapple ambrosia? Cheesy garlic fries?" Then he bobbed his head back and forth to the thud of the beat.

"You look like a sea anemone," I said, because he did with his feet flat on the floor and his poofy blond hair waving.

"You're just jealous." Harry bobbed some more, and I found that I was smiling, too.

"You could be right," I said. "God, Harry, I'm so happy for—"

"Whoaaa, *Harry-Fairy!*" squeaked a reedy little voice nearby, and Harry staggered in place and went still. Way down in my chest, the old worry flared anew, a brush fire I really thought I'd contained, threatening my ribs and filling my lungs with smoke.

Prancing toward us, weaving between tables, came two black-haired boys. The older of the two, maybe ten, wore skater shorts belted halfway down his thighs, plus unlaced high-top sneakers with the backs crushed and the sides sagging and the tongues dangling, like strangled dogs he was kicking. The younger boy, seven at the oldest, had a red construction-paper crown on his head that he'd clearly made himself. His expression was kinder.

"Students," Harry murmured to me, recovering his balance, at least, though he couldn't seem to get his smile back in place.

"Stop it," I said, because somehow, I already knew. Something about the tone of the voices, the lack of . . . not respect, really, because there was a little of that. But deference. "It's alright, Harry," I said. "It's fine. Really. It's good."

"Harry-Fairy, I'm the Lava King," said the younger boy, and stomped his feet, which were bare below his sandy bathing suit and long, brandless T-shirt. Because of his pudginess and the crown on his head and the way his black eyes, lit with citronella-orange, danced around the room and up to Harry's face and down again like twin fireflies, he looked even younger than he was.

"Who's the semi-babe?" said the older boy.

"Hi, Teddy," Harry said to the younger kid, though he kept glancing at me. "Ryan. This is my cousin Mimi."

"Your hair's orange," Ryan said.

"Your knee's broken," I answered, executing a quick grab-and-twist which ended with my sneaker against the inside edge of his patella. I let the kid go, and he spun around and glared at me. But when I didn't smile, didn't smirk, just nodded at him, he broke abruptly into a grin.

"Harry-Fairy, are you going to come to class again for the no-litter game?" said Teddy, and Harry flinched, and I had an inkling, a memory, a sudden nauseous feeling.

"You boys . . ." Harry glanced my way again but not meeting my glare. I tapped my foot in exasperation.

"Want to lose at pool?" I said to the older boy. "You play pool?"

"He's good," said Teddy.

"I am," said Ryan.

"Let's go."

They broke off in tandem, racing around the bar for pool cues and then into the back room. Harry and I followed, more slowly.

"You're a janitor," I said quietly. "Right?"

"Don't be mad," Harry whispered. "Gardener, actually. I'm the school gardener."

"I'm only mad because you think it makes any difference to me."

"How'd you know?"

I shrugged. "Who calls their teacher Harry-Fairy? I don't know. It's just . . . the way kids talk to maintenance guys. I'm fresh out of high school, remember."

"I remember," Harry said. "Congratulations, by the way. On graduating, I mean." If he'd gone to touch my hand, I would have let him, but he didn't, and I wasn't going to do it for him.

The back room of Puhi's Den turned out to be a den. Dark red carpeting lined not only the floors, but the walls. The only light came from twin shaded lamps suspended over the two pool tables, whose surfaces were long and green and so perfectly maintained that they reflected the light like the goldfish ponds outside. A single rectangular window space—glassless, like the openings in the main room—overlooked a thicket of palms. Beyond them, beyond the pink-roofed cabanas and the luau grove and the cliffside, I could see a sliver of ocean lit white by the moon.

"They actually let kids play on those tables?" I asked.

"These kids are good pool players," Harry said. "Ryan, especially."

"Still."

"Their parents are pastry chefs here."

I put my hand on the nearest table, and its felt, thick and soft and weirdly warm, rose to meet my palm like fur. "Still," I said.

Though I couldn't say so to Harry—he was way too sensitive—the little revelation about his job bothered me more than I wanted to admit. Not because of the job; it didn't matter, I'd meant what I said. But the lying gave me that familiar prickly feeling.

"Straight pool?" Ryan said, balls racked expertly on the nearest table, pool cue cocked at his side like a speargun.

"How about stripes and solids?" said Harry, glancing at me and then quickly away. He really was a goddamn bloodhound, I thought. He could smell someone doubting him miles away. "You and Teddy against Me and Mi?"

"Me and Mi?" Ryan echoed, adding sneer.

"Well, that's her name," said Harry.

"No it isn't," I muttered, more cruelly than I intended, and the boys looked at me, and Harry didn't. "Break," I told Ryan.

"No slop," said the kid. "Call it all."

Dropping into position with no hesitation and more command than he should have been able to manage, given his size, Ryan popped the stick like a piston, and the cue ball shot down the table and shattered the rack with a smack. Two balls—one stripe, one solid—dropped in opposing corner pockets. "Six. Side," Ryan said, and knocked down the six.

Suddenly, with a giggle I hardly recognized, Harry dropped into a crouch next to the corner pocket Ryan was now studying and planted his face on the rubber ring behind it.

"Hey," said Ryan. "Move."

Harry snapped his lips open, popped them shut like a gulping fish. "Shoot," he said. "Dare you."

"Harry, get up," I said, because Ryan would dare, there was no question.

"Teddy the Lava King'll have to make me. It's a team game." Harry looked at me, dropped one eyelid closed and opened it again.

"Was that a wink?" I said. "Do people do that?"

Harry winked again, and Teddy the Lava King sprang forward to push him out of the way just as Ryan rammed his stick home and rocketed the four ball straight for Harry's teeth. The ball slammed into the back of the pocket, right where Harry had been, and lipped out, and Ryan said, "Shit!" as Harry fell prone on his back, just in time, snared Teddy, and flipped him over his knees into a soft, butt-first landing in the thick red carpet.

"Our turn," Harry said from the ground, grinning.

"Cheater," said Ryan.

"That was funny, Harry-Fairy," said Teddy the Lava King, and smiled at Harry.

Harry sprang to his feet and melted into the shadows at the back of the room. I saw him fiddling in his pockets, punching buttons on a machine against the wall, and Janet Jackson came on, the one about her slipping her girlfriend out of her new black dress.

"Appropriate choice there, Har," I said, glancing at the seven-year-old at my feet, but Harry just bobbed, grinned, snatched the pool cue from Ryan's hands, and stuck it between his legs like a broomstick he was going to command to life and ride. His face had gone red, his eyes wild, as though he'd somehow willed himself drunk, but you couldn't do anything but laugh at him, with him. Even Ryan was laughing as Harry vaulted up to the table, leaned over it, and the sky caved in.

That really is what it seemed like. As if a giant scrap of the moon-streaked black out there had torn loose and tumbled through the glassless windows into the room. Harry ducked hard, raking an ugly furrow in the felt and whacking his chin against the edge of the table, and I stumbled back several steps with my hands up blocking my face, and Teddy the Lava King started screaming and wouldn't stop.

For a few seconds, the thing wheeled around the room, sweeping up to the ceiling and down over Harry's head and smacking, finally, against the hood of the lamp over our pool table and sticking there, twitching, like a manta ray trying to shrug the night back over its shoulders. All of us froze, staring.

"That," said Harry, straightening slowly, backing away and swiping his hand across his hair where he'd been skimmed, "is the biggest . . . what is it? Is that a bat?"

"I hate it," Teddy whimpered from the floor, scuttling away from the table with his eyes locked on the lamp. "I hate it, I hate it, I *hate* it."

Like a kite catching a wind current, the thing blew off the lamp and tumbled toward me as I laughed and dropped to my knees, then straight for Teddy, who screamed and batted at it and may even have hit it because it tipped in the air, sailed up the wall and lit against it, swinging slightly as if caught in a web, although I could not imagine the spider that could hold it. If that spider exists, though, I thought, remembering the dolphins beneath me in the water and the outrageous gardenias blooming everywhere like blazing, newborn stars, it exists here.

"Please get it away," Teddy whined.

"Shut up, baby," said Ryan.

"That's the biggest—" Harry started again.

I cut him off. "It's a moth," I said, stunned, still crouching. "Jesus Christ, that's a moth." It had to have been two feet across, maybe more, all black except for twin, eye-shaped green spots at the edge of both wings. As it hung, unnaturally still, I got a glimpse of its body, long and fat like a beetle's. And I saw its antennae, which were surprisingly thin, tiny little feelers probing the air like a baby's fingers, and a sudden, sweet-sad taste seeped into my chest, and I felt like a little girl.

"Harry, you gotta make it go," Teddy said. He was crying.

"It won't hurt you." I rose and moved toward him. "Right?"

This last bit I directed at Harry, and he grinned at me, proud, as though he'd grown the moth himself, produced it out of thin air like a magician. "Right," he said. "Come on, stand up, Te—"

The thing swung off the wall again, diving down on Ryan and sending him scurrying for cover under a nearby drink table while Teddy wailed and I just stared and Harry snatched up his stick like a badminton racquet and swung at it.

"Don't," I snapped, and Harry swung again as he stepped close to Teddy.

"Shush, Mimes," Harry said. "I'm just keeping it off my boy, here." He looked flushed, as though something had been stoked inside him.

I said, "Harry, *don't!*" one more time, and Teddy screamed, and the moth pinwheeled toward the window but then arced around again, tiny feelers waving, stretching for our hair, the light, and Harry swung and burst it like a piñata.

"*Dude!*" Ryan yelled, half-laughing from under the table as bits of wing and body rained to the carpet around him.

"*Goddamn it, Harry,*" I snarled, staggering and grabbing the edge of the pool table and blinking furiously as tears I hadn't expected and didn't understand flooded my eyes.

Silence engulfed us. The jukebox had gone quiet. Teddy was too stunned to shriek anymore, and Ryan's mouth had come unhinged, hanging halfway between gape and grin. Harry stood near Teddy, not moving, pool cue clutched in his hand. The clumps of black and green clinging near its tip might have been chalk dust.

"Amelia," he whispered.

"Shut up," I said. "Don't talk to me." The silence, I noticed, seemed to have washed all the way through Puhi's Den, because the other room had gone quiet, too. It was like being shut in a vault, losing the sense and sound of the world.

Dropping into a crouch, I stared down at the moth's savaged body, one wing, the eyelet brilliant green against the black. It looked mounted to the carpet. Then it twitched.

"Oh shit," I said. The wing twitched again, brushed the ground, beat against it, and the half-a-moth began to spin slowly, horribly, almost hopping along the floor like a decapitated wind-up toy. "Oh, little thing. Harry, kill it."

"What?" he said. "Wh—no."

"Harry, you fuckball, get over here and kill this thing. It can't live this way."

"I can't."

"Oh my God, you're such an *asshole!*" I hissed. "You want it to suffer some more? You think it's funny? You and that little budding dickhead over there?" I gestured, furious, toward Ryan, glanced down at the half-moth jerking along the floor. My voice went quiet, I didn't even think he could hear me, didn't want him to, really, or maybe I did. "After all, Har. Just another dead thing no one will miss. Yeah?"

In one terrible movement, Harry stepped forward and slammed the pool cue down on the floor, then did it again as I squeezed my eyes shut and Ryan said, "Oooh," and Teddy the Lava King sobbed. When I opened my eyes, Harry was staring at me, leaning on the pool cue as if it were a staff, blond hair wild on his head. Oedipus, at the moment of self-revelation. Tremors rippled through his arms and legs, one after another, earthquake and aftershock way down in the core of his being. Because he knew I hated him.

Because I really did, for a moment. Had. And he knew it. "Harry," I said, gathering myself, "I—"

"What on God's green earth is *wrong with you?*" a voice I almost recognized screamed, and another figure came flying into the room, this one blond and too thin and green eyed, and then I knew her. Laptop skeleton-woman from the plane. Which had landed, I realized in astonishment, less than six hours ago.

The woman barged right up to Harry, snatched the pool cue out of his hands, and hurled it to the ground. Harry rocked, trembled again, and I thought he might collapse.

"Hey," I said, standing, but both Harry and the woman ignored me.

"Do you have any idea where you are?" the woman snarled, all but spitting in her fury. "Do you have any sense of anything in the world at all except you? You're in *their* world," she said, gesturing to the puddle of moth on the carpet. "This is paradise. Maybe the last one. And your reaction to seeing something as gorgeous and strange and alive as that creature is to smash it to pieces?"

I waited for Harry to rouse himself, explain, apologize, anything, but his eyes and lips were quivering as though he was about to jiggle to pieces.

"He didn't mean—"

The woman spun to me. "He crushed it. After dismembering it. For fun."

"He was putting it out of—"

"Are you insane? Who *are* you? You don't belong here. You or your cousin, if that's really who you are."

I was so focused on diverting her attention from Harry that I didn't notice what she'd said at first. I felt like I was distracting a shark in a blood frenzy. "The little boy was upset. Harry was—"

The woman whirled to Teddy, who was still sobbing next to the table but alert enough to cringe back from her glare.

"He did wrong, Teddy," the woman said, and I understood, finally, that she knew them. Knew us all. "He couldn't have done more wrong. Don't ever do what he did. Don't ever be like him. Ever, ever, ever." The glare swept across me, back to Harry. "Give me my goddamn truck keys. We'll see if I can stand to have you working for me anymore on Monday."

I blinked, opened my mouth to say something, scream back, but said nothing. Because if I screamed anything, I was worried I'd do it at Harry. I didn't want to turn on him. I was all he had. But he'd lied all over the place for the thousandth time, and this time there was just me here, so none of his traditional excuses and reasons applied. Never in my life had I been so furious. "You heard her," I said to my cousin, hating my voice because it was my mother's. "Give the woman her keys."

For a second, I thought I was going to have to jam my hands in Harry's pockets and get them for him. But he managed, somehow.

"Come with me, boys," the woman said. "Let's go find your parents."

"Ms. Jones," Harry said, "I'm—"

"Yes. Well. Does that feel good enough? To you?"

She stalked off, and the boys jerked after her like coupled boxcars, leaving me and my cousin and the moth-bits to the dark of the den, the moon-soaked sky, the whistling in the palm trees as the tradewinds whispered through them.

3

"It's time," I heard Harry whisper, dimly, as though across a thousand miles of ocean. "Mimi, wake up." On the third or fourth time, I opened my eyes.

Sometime during the night, I'd twisted Harry's lone blanket underneath my shoulders to insulate myself just a little more from the cold stone floor of the converted garden shed my cousin called home. Wriggling out of it now felt like freeing myself from a cocoon, except that all I'd become, I suspected, was sadder, blanker, and older. Do those things always come together?

"Hurry," Harry said again. "It's time."

"For what?" I said, standing, staring at him. He wore the same shorts as yesterday, same Hawaiian shirt, although the colors seemed to have faded overnight like ink on an old postcard.

"I told you. You have to hit it at just the right moment. It only happens when everything's just right."

"Which is clearly how everything is this morning." The words were bitter as battery acid in my mouth.

"Just get your suit on. Please."

"You go. I'm tired."

But the expression on Harry's face—lizard eyes ballooning under his lenses, cheeks seeming to deflate as though I'd suctioned all the oxygen out of him—kept me from flopping back to the floor.

"Mimi, please. It's why I brought you here."

"I brought me here," I said, but I was already past him, squeezing into the tiny bathroom humped onto the back of the shed like a U-Haul trailer.

"We'll be swimming," he told me.

I shut the door and dressed. My swimsuit, still wet from the day before, felt sticky and freezing against my stomach and chest, as if I were sliding into someone else's skin. I got my teeth brushed, my hair knotted back. "Still red," I said to the mirror, thinking about going home, seeing my sensei, taking my brown-belt test sometime this coming August, packing up my room bit by bit while my mother watched and cried a little from the doorway. Ten weeks from now, I would be in Santa Cruz by myself. College girl. I turned, bumped my knee on the edge of the toilet, swore, and saw the black sky through the tiny square of window perched eye-high on the wall.

"What the hell time is it?" I called.

"Almost four," said Harry. "Hurry."

The shed sat in a hedge-enfolded corner of the screaming woman's lot—she'd given him housing as well as work—and as we sloshed through the grass, I saw Harry glance through the wet white mist toward the glassed-in sun porch that ran the whole length of the two-story white clapboard main house like a moat.

"She sleeps out there sometimes," Harry said.

"Is this place walking distance?"

"It's all the way across the island."

"Whose truck are we going to steal now?"

After that, Harry stopped speaking for a while. Minutes later, in the same green truck we'd used yesterday, we were flying down the pothole-riven road out of what passed for the ritzy part of Lanai, called Haole Camp because that's where the haoles lived. Even Harry. All the houses were white, too.

"She gave you the keys back?" I asked, mostly to break the silence. Harry just stared out the windshield, didn't look at me, and made a whistling sound every now and then through his pursed mouth as though trying to hypnotize himself. I wasn't used to my cousin when he wasn't wheedling.

"I know where she keeps the spare set," he said flatly. "I went and got them before I woke you."

"That's great, Har. Good for you."

For once, he didn't take the bait, just drove and breathed. I think I had my first inkling, right then, tickling across my ribs on little ant feet. But I didn't recognize it.

In the mist, Lanai City proper looked more like a tide pool than a town. I saw low green huts clinging to their rocky plots like barnacles, their backs mottled and sunken, the yards around them scattered with the broken skeletons of bicycle frames and divided by surprising bursts of spiny purple and yellow flowers like colonies of sea urchins. On a leaning picnic table in one yard, I saw a solitary man—an islander—sipping something steaming from a plain white mug and reading a newspaper. Other than him, I saw no one at all.

In a matter of moments, the town fell away, and what was left of all that lush green seemed to seep out of the grass into the surrounding blackness as though we'd reached the edge of a painting. I saw a tilting cyclone fence, a sign reading *Garden of the Gods* with an arrow pointing up a steep hillside path, a gate, and giant boulders bunched in the rolling fields, all tilted in the same direction like fossilized herds of wild horses, and just as we crested the ridge at the top of the island, I saw real horses, still as the stones, forelocks raised in identical poses, noses down, as though they were paying homage to the ocean. As though they'd just crawled out of it, sprouted lungs and hooves, become what they were.

"Stop," I said.

"Can't," said Harry, and drove on.

"I'm trying to tell you I see what you mean."

"What are you talking about?"

"It does feel kind of ghostly or Godly or something up here."

"You haven't seen," Harry said. "You will."

For a brief while, we'd been rolling along the flat top of the ridge, and now we reached the other side, the downhill slope, and at last, for a moment, Harry stopped the truck. I stared.

It was like another island entirely, another planet. On this side of Lanai, the hillsides that spilled down to the ocean had been buffeted and burned completely free of grass and color. I saw a few stunted trees, rocky outcroppings, colorless moss lying flat on the ground as if some of the morning mist had left a residue there. I half-believed I could see boulders steaming as they bubbled newly formed from the earth. Is there even air down there, I found myself wondering? Gravity?

Before I was ready, Harry started the truck forward again. His periodic, ritualized breathing had slowed, stopped seeming so premeditated. Now he just looked calm in a way I'd never seen. At the bottom of the mountain, where the road leveled, the pavement gave out, but Harry just bounced us along over the dirt through stands of scrawny fender-high bushes that bore no leaves and seemed to have no space for them amid their snarls of branches. They looked like sketches for bushes. Practice. I thought about the dolphins and giant moths and people playing ukuleles on the grassy luau grounds back by the hotel, the pineapple groves and wild horses on the hillsides. Taking this drive was like traveling backward through evolution. Which meant that the ocean ahead of us wouldn't be ocean yet, really, just a swirl of black gas and space dust.

"We were going to sleep in her house, weren't we?" I said

abruptly, jamming my hands against the ceiling of the truck to keep my head from banging against it.

Harry's eyes stayed trained down the beams of our headlights onto the rutted dirt before us. "I know you don't believe me, Amelia," he said in his new, expressionless voice. "But she was going to let me. I was supposed to be house-sitting. For Marion Jones. She's the principal at the grade school where I work."

"Hopefully *still* work," I said. I couldn't help it. I was furious about the preceding night and the endless lying. For once, I actually wanted him to wheedle.

"She wasn't supposed to be back for a week, yet."

"You were going to tell me it was yours, though," I said, and for the second time in twelve hours, tears formed in my eyes without warning or explanation. I almost reached for my cousin's hand.

"I'd rather you thought I lived there than the garden shed. Yeah. It's true," Harry said, in his robot-drone.

"Goddamn you, Harry." I turned to the window so that he couldn't see me crying.

Humps formed in the land around us, round and flat and blackened, as though they'd been in a fire. Can emptiness burn, I wondered? The perspective seemed all wrong, the road tilted to one side, the earth heaving. Overhead, the first watery yellow light trickled through the clouds like iodine tracing a vein.

A few minutes later, our wheels began to spin and slip as the dirt softened into sand, and finally, between two leaning black mounds that closed the view on either side of us, Harry switched off the truck.

"It's not far," he said, and now there was at least a hint of something in his voice. Eagerness? Hunger? "Hurry. Take this."

From under his seat, he withdrew flippers, a mask, and a snorkel.

"Your ship's sunk?" I asked, surprised.

"Can't sink," Harry said. Without waiting, he hopped from the truck and started fast down the dirt, his own flippers draped over one shoulder like a single folded wing.

As soon as I was out, I heard the ocean. It sounded restless, rolling and hissing and slapping at the land. The dawn breeze pressed my sodden swimsuit to my chest, sealing in the cold. Harry had already gotten way ahead, so I scrambled after him, arms tight against me to keep in whatever heat I still generated. It was the light more than the air that made it seem so chilly here, I thought. Soon, the bushes began creeping into my path, uncurling their spongy, leafless branches into the air. They looked like anemones that had spilled off the reef onto dry land. I found that I didn't want to touch them. The thought of those branches curling, drawing my finger toward some hidden mouth, made me shudder. I stepped between and around them, quickened my pace, and stopped when I hit the camp.

Despite the deadness around me and the fact that Harry was practically sprinting away, now, I found myself standing still. I couldn't help it.

Mostly, I stared at the sheds, three-walled, wide open on the side that faced me. The walls themselves were wooden, black, well on their way to decomposing, as though they'd been lying on the ocean floor. I saw two circular stone fire rings, the wagon end of some sort of rig, and a single, stone tureen, two feet deep at least, tipped over on its side in the dirt. I stepped off the path while Little Red Riding Hood warnings whispered in my ears in my mother's voice.

Moving amongst those dilapidated, rotting buildings, their window holes gaping, their roofs caved in, was like diving on a shipwreck. The air felt heavier, and what light there was spiraled down in thin gray shafts. I tried to imagine people living here, having a Saturday-night dance around the fire circle, and found that I couldn't. What could they have been doing here, anyway? After a few minutes among the stillness and shadows, the place began to feel more like a natural formation than a ruin. And it smelled like the ocean.

I don't know how long I lingered there, but when I shook free of my trance, I realized that I couldn't see Harry anymore and that he hadn't called for me. Scrambling back to the path, swatting away all sorts of swooping, black-winged thoughts, I marched myself up the last ridge, and right as I reached the top and saw Shipwreck Beach for the first time, I heard the sound.

At first it was a single tone, low and long and round. If not for the daylight, I might have mistaken it for the cry of an owl. Then it went lower, got lonelier. Whale song, I thought? Some thousand-mile wind screaming down the Pacific to fill this cove and ring it? Then I stopped speculating, just stood and listened until, finally, after a long, long time, it died away, leaving a sort of void in the center of my eardrum, as though it had hollowed out a channel there. I stumbled off the ridge, looked over the water, and saw the wreck.

It lay two hundred yards from shore, maybe less, propped straight up in the roiling surf, so improbably still that it looked projected on the mist, barely even solid. Its gray, featureless steel sides reflected nothing, and the sea spray from the waves smashing against the bow slid over it easily, naturally, as though over sharkskin. As though the ship could breathe it.

"Harry!" I shouted, and then I saw him hunched on a piece of driftwood at the edge of the water, sliding into his flippers. He looked up and saw me. For a second, he seemed almost surprised that I was there. Then, hesitantly—as though we hadn't seen each other in months, and last night had never happened—he smiled and waved. I started toward him, staring around.

For miles, it seemed, in either direction, driftwood littered the sand, leaned against the boulders, rotted into pulpy puddles and drained into the ocean. Beyond the sand, long, wriggling snakes of white water curled around and bit at themselves, smashed on underwater rocks, shot up in the air and got sucked under by the current.

Not until I was right on top of Harry, watching him strip off his shirt and flex his feet in the flippers, did it occur to me to wonder what he thought we were doing.

"We're not swimming out there," I said, and for the second time, understanding surfaced in my sleep-fuzzed, sound-rattled brain and sank again.

"I am," he told me, and stood. Where he'd been sitting, a single tiny black crab poked a pincer out of a notch in the wood, edged forward, then scuttled into the sand. "I'm hoping you'll come. I saved this until you came." He lifted his eyes almost to mine, dropped them again. "It's the reason I wanted you to come."

"Why?" I snapped. "You want to pretend it's yours? Maybe you're establishing a school there for shipwrecked sailors? Now that you're a teacher and all?"

"You're the only—" Harry said quietly. Then the sound started again, and he went quiet and closed his eyes.

For a few seconds, I looked all around me, trying to locate its source, and then I went still, too. Mating call? Mourning wail? I couldn't tell, didn't much care. It filled my head, my skin, as though a second being had climbed in there with me, and it made me warmer, but also sadder, and I wanted to run, and I wanted to cry.

"Harry, what is that?" I whispered, a good thirty seconds or so after it had faded away again.

"It's coming from the ship."

"Are you sure?" I wasn't sure. It might have been. Dazed, I watched the water roll over my cousin's feet, his too-thin ankles as he stepped off the edge of the land. "Not even cold," he said, and looked back at me, just once. He continued forward up to his knees, stumbled on some underwater rock, and almost pitched face first into the surf.

"Just wait a fucking second," I said, shaking myself free of whatever it was that held me spellbound. I slammed my fins down, shoved my feet into them, dropped my shorts and shirt, perched the mask and snorkel on my forehead, and duckwalked down to the shoreline.

"It looks trickier than it is," he said, studying the whirls of gray green water, the eruptions of spray between us and the wreck.

"Right," I murmured.

I watched my cousin sink to his knees in the water, lower his mask. "It's shallow all the way out, supposedly," he said. "Coral, right up near the surface. That's what the mask is for. Don't get scraped, it'll hurt like hell." With a flip of his fins, he kicked into the churning, circling current. I didn't let myself think. I kicked in after him.

For fifteen strokes or so, it really was easier than it looked. The water, maybe five feet at its deepest, tugged and dragged at me, not hard, which shouldn't have fooled me. But I was too busy watching the coral fan out beneath me, miniature mountains and yellow peninsulas and rolling plains like the countryside on the model railroad set I'd had as a kid, and that Harry had broken. Schools of silver reef fish streamed over the landscape and all around us. A black turtle rose from the bottom like a lost balloon, floated over my right shoulder, studied me, and broke off into the shadows. The snap-current that caught me came from nowhere, swept me so fast and so hard into the coral outcropping on my right that for one screaming, irrational second, I thought I'd been sharkbit.

"*Shit!*" I gargled, and salt water streamed around my mouthpiece into my mouth, and for some reason, that settled me, or at least woke me up some more. I coughed, gagged, kicked hard, and felt another scrape-and-rip along my left thigh. One more yank of the undertow, and I was off the reef, floating free. I caught a glimpse of my blood in the water, a red, wispy vapor trail, and then I was flung forward, eyes everywhere, arms and hands and feet slapping and flailing as I lurched out to sea.

I made no more mistakes after that. I twisted, tucked, flowed like an octopus between boulders of coral and then lunged in a new direction, half-fighting the current, half-riding it, and right before I hit the sandbar and realized I could stand, I found myself wondering how I was going to look up long enough to locate the ship. The scrape on my stomach panicked me at first. I looked down expecting to have been torn wide open and real-ized that nothing was hurt, that the touch had been granular and gentle, and I jammed my feet down.

"God," I said when I found I could speak.

Harry, expressionless, pulled me to my feet, his eyes over my shoulder. I turned to see where he was looking.

Twenty feet away, just off the edge of the strip of sand where Harry and I stood, the marooned ship towered above us, blacking out the dawn, dead center in a caldron of crashing, crushing, cascading water. Up close, its steel didn't look smooth or gray but pitted, streaked with wide, wet, jagged bands of red and rust orange and silver, like the seething, banded clouds of Jupiter.

"What *is* this?" I whispered. "How did it get here?"

"No one knows." Harry spoke quietly, too, which made it hard to hear over the roaring water.

I waited, expecting another story like the one about Pu'upehe. But Harry just stared at the ship, mouth moving as if he were praying.

"How long has it been here?"

Harry shrugged. "The guidebooks call it a Liberty ship. Built during World War II. The history guy at school told me President Roosevelt called them 'Dreadful-looking things.'"

"No dummy, he."

"Only it isn't a Liberty ship. That's the thing, Mimi." He was still all but whispering, and now he began to edge down the sandbar. "A guy a couple years ago, some kind of ship enthusiast, called some foundation in San Francisco, and they said this couldn't be a Liberty ship. And it doesn't have a number on it. And no one saw it come or can even pinpoint when it arrived. It just appeared here one day. And it won't sink. The Navy's tried three times. They can't get it off the reef and down. And it won't rust, either. Not like it should." He was looking down into the water churning against the sandbar. "This shouldn't be so hard. Look, you just angle left, right there . . ."

"Look what I did to my goddamn leg," I said, studying the red rent that ran from my hip straight down the tendon to my knee. Little coral spines stuck from the skin. In the weak morning light, they seemed to wiggle like little parasites. I began to pick at one, and then realized, finally, what he'd said.

"Harry." I hobbled up behind him and put my hands on his shoulders. They were wet, still powerful under the flab, and I could feel his heart shuddering like some over-revved engine. Whatever the quiet was in his voice, it didn't signify calm. "Look at the waves. Look how hard they hit the ship. We can't—"

"There's a ladder near the stern. I'm pretty sure that's what he said. Look, one good surge and you're past the danger zone."

"That's what *who* said? That's . . ." I started, then stopped. I watched the water erupt out of hollows in itself and explode against the steel hull in a deafening, never-ending cannonade. "Harry, I don't want to die."

"Then don't." Harry turned to me and smiled suddenly. "I love you, Mimi." And real understanding dawned, at last. I knew what I was doing here, and why he'd insisted I come, and why he'd waited for me.

"You son of a bitch," I said, "Don't you fucking dare." And then he leapt. The water sucked him straight down and swept him out of sight around the side of the ship. I didn't see or hear him hit, which didn't mean he hadn't. And I wouldn't know if he had, I realized, because I couldn't see where he was.

But he didn't want me to drown, I thought. He'd wanted me to come because he was too fucking much of a coward to kill himself by himself. But my dying was something he could never live with, and I knew it. I didn't stop to examine the obvious flaw in my logic. There wasn't time.

Compared to the swim from shore, shooting past the ship proved stunningly easy. The second my feet hit water, I was catapulted forward, screaming toward the point of the bow and then wide of it, straight along the hull, rimming the lip of a trough of water that dove against the half-exposed, rust-eaten keel. What remained was simply to stick out my hands and snag the posts of a long steel ladder as they flew past, which I did, my knees banging against the ship and the underside of one arm scraping hard as I wedged it on the bottom rung and dragged myself out of the water. Harry was already fifteen steps above me, headed directly up the hull. Like someone who'd long ago spotted the ledge he would jump from.

"Goddamn you, *wait up!*" I howled, but I doubt he heard me. I shoved upward with my legs and started climbing, slowing only to dab at the blood streaming down my side. Determined as Harry was, I was faster, and soon I was only a few steps below him. He was panting, but still climbing. "Harry, stop!" I screamed up at him.

He did, momentarily, glancing down at me. "You're fine," he said.

"I know I'm fine, I just—"

"Let's talk up top, yeah? I don't like hanging on this thing." Up he went, ignoring my snarl of protest.

The whole climb probably took five minutes, maybe less. It only lasted that long because my feet kept sliding on the slick rungs, and once, two-thirds of the way up, just at the point where the bow began to bell out so that I had to climb tilted backward, I glanced down and saw the surf sliding back over the rocks and coral beneath me like lips over bared teeth, and I couldn't move for a while. When I finally managed to look up again, Harry was gone.

I had a moment of panic, jammed myself tight against the ladder as I imagined my cousin's body screaming past me on its way down. Tiny cirrus clouds of spray floated far beneath me. I felt like Jack, right at the top of his beanstalk, only stupider. Jack's idiot cousin, who followed wherever he went.

"Harry, help me," I shouted when I reached the rustless metal railing that ringed the deck of the ship and realized I was going to have to jump a little from the top step of the ladder to hoist myself over it. But Harry didn't come, and I couldn't stay where I was, so I leapt, caught my hips on the rail, tumbled over onto the deck, and lay there, gasping, in the creeping daylight. Immediately, by force of habit, my lungs fell into their kata rhythm, regulating themselves, and when I stood, I was not shaking at all.

The first thing I noticed—the most alarming thing—was the quiet. It wasn't quite silence, because the wind whistled over the bulkheads and between the truck-sized wooden and metal containers jammed into virtually every available inch of deck space. But I couldn't hear any birds, and I couldn't hear the ocean.

"I bet we're fifteen stories up," Harry said, appearing from behind one of the containers. "More." His hair was flying every which way, and his skin seemed almost translucent, like a baby's. He hardly seemed capable of walking, let alone lying or killing a man or scaling this ship or hurling himself off of it. The eagerness in his voice was quieter than it had been as we entered Puhi's Den last night, but also less explicable, and therefore scarier.

"Is that a tank?" I said, shoving him aside so I could see past him. Buying time, so I could figure out how to talk him down. Fifteen feet away, a hulking real-live tank hunkered on its treads, gun nozzle extended up and out at a forty-five-degree angle like the neck of a dinosaur.

"Come on," said Harry, and I couldn't think of anything to do but follow him.

For a while, we explored in silence, mostly together, because I wouldn't let Harry get more than five feet from me. We touched the treads of the tank as though they were paws, scrambled over knee-high thickets of coiled rope and the valved tops of what might have been cisterns full of water or oil dug into the deck, stood at the foot of the mizzenmast and stared up through the skeleton wires at the sky going blue. It was like wandering in a pueblo, or through the ruins of some medieval castle somewhere. People had been here, okay, but their lives were unimaginable to me. The sound, when it came, seemed softer, somehow, than it had from the land, and so natural in that place that I didn't notice it starting, didn't consciously register it until my cousin fell to his knees beside me.

"Oh, wow," he said, closed his eyes and bowed his head.

It was like a loon call but longer, lonelier. It trilled up, intensified, and there were near-consonants in it, soft r's and y's, as though whatever it was had known language once and forgotten it. The pitch rose toward screaming, and my hands flew to my ears as Harry bent forward into the face of the rising sun like a Moslem praying at daybreak, and then the sound sighed out.

"What do you think that is?" Harry said, after a long time. "It's amazing, isn't it?"

I shook my head. "I don't know. Wind? The way the water hits the boat? It's weird."

"It's more than that." He was crying, I realized. Bowing his head and crying. "It's alive."

"Harry." I knelt next to him. I held my hand between his shoulder blades while sobs racked him, and I waited. But the sobs kept coming, and I felt panic again in my stomach and lungs, and my fingers curled into a fist against his back. "Harry, listen. It'll be okay."

"What are you talking about?" he hissed, through another explosion of tears.

"It will. It will, it will, it will. It's not too late."

"Mimi, that's the stupidest—"

"I want you to take me home," I snapped, because I knew what I'd said was idiotic. I didn't have anything good to say. I just wanted him to come with me. "Harry? I want you to take me home."

When he finally looked up, his eyes were red, and his voice came from far away.

"You go ahead," he said.

"You come. Come on." I put my hands under his elbows, tried to lift him, and he came with surprising ease.

"You feel it, too, don't you, Mimi?"

"Feel what?"

"It's . . . a resting place. You can tell. A place to rest. A magic place."

Now there were tears in my eyes. They stung when I blinked and made me cry more. I had nowhere to lead us but back toward the ladder. "Harry. Come rest with me. It's not too late. There's still time to put things right. Some things, anyway."

"You're right," Harry said dreamily. Too peacefully. His smile was scarier than his tears, but he let me lead him. I kept moving forward, not looking at his face anymore. I just pulled him behind me. This was it, I thought. I was Orpheus, on the journey home. If I looked back, he'd know I doubted him. If I looked back, he'd be gone.

"It isn't all your fault, Harry. It never has been. And even if it has, you're still here. You're twenty-three years old. You owe the people you hurt. You owe yourself. You owe *me*, goddamn you. You can still prove my mother wrong. And your mother. And all of them. You can still prove me right."

Harry said nothing, just went where I tugged him like a balloon tied to my wrist. I reached the railing, kept my breathing steady, forced the trembling in my legs to stillness. I had a decision to make. I couldn't carry him, obviously. I could make him go first and watch him leap if he decided to do it. Or I could go ahead and trust him to follow.

Either was better than standing here, halfway out of the world already, marooned offshore and above it.

"Harry," I said, turning to face him, pinning his eyes with my own.

"Are you crying?" He actually sounded startled.

"I'm going down now. I want you to promise you're coming."

"Hey." He shrugged himself at least part of the way free of his stupor. He smiled that new, scary smile again. "Nowhere else to go."

"I want you to promise you're coming down on the ladder," I snapped. "All the way to the water. Got it?"

His eyes slipped from mine toward the horizon.

"Harry, I swear to God. I will not forgive you this. I can't. I came to prison, and I came to Lanai. I swam to the dead-wife rock, and I climbed this ship, and did everything else you asked."

"I didn't bring you here for me," he said, not looking at me. "Jeez, Mimi. I just thought you'd want to see it."

I couldn't even make sense of that. He was coming, or he was jumping, and either way, I couldn't help him anymore. I draped my legs over the side of the ship and had a sickening moment hanging there when my feet couldn't find the ladder and then they did, and I was standing. I edged myself around so that I was facing the hull, careful to look neither down nor up. If Harry jumped, I refused to watch him. I was ten rungs down, clinging to the metal, waiting, every second, for the whistle of Harry's body plunging past me, the thump of it shattering on the rocks below, when I felt the metal groan and knew my cousin was on the ladder.

"Took you long enough," I shouted, giddy with relief. I didn't stop, didn't look up, dropped down another few steps, and the sound broke over us once more.

It seemed softer this time. Almost comforting, and as it slid lower, it seemed to work its way into my blood like a purr. It's perfect, I thought. Just right. The last mournful chord for the first part of Harry's life. I'd gotten him off the ship. I might even be able to get him off Lanai and back to the mainland. Even when the sound intensified, the same way it had before, it felt bearable, almost musical. I never had the urge to cover my ears, and couldn't have, anyway, I wasn't taking my hands off the ladder. It's just the world, I told myself. It's just the way the world sounds. I closed my eyes, bowing my head as the sound fattened, distorted, and, at last, sank to nothing, like a long, expiring breath. I opened my eyes and glanced up just in time to see Harry's legs disappear back over the top of the railing onto the ship.

"Where are you *going?*" I screamed, not really expecting an answer, but Harry's head reappeared instantly, his hair shooting off his head in flares and prominences like a sun going nova, his features all but bleached out.

"What?" he said.

"What are you doing?"

"Didn't you hear it? It's stuck in the hold."

I shook my head, slammed the edge of my hand against the nearest rung of ladder and rang it.

"It's down below," Harry said again.

"What is, Harry? What? Empty ship?"

"You tell me, Mimi. Go ahead. I want to know what you think it is."

"Who cares? I'll tell you what it isn't. It isn't the ghost of the man Randy Lynne ran over. It isn't either one of our moms. It isn't God. And it isn't me. It's the wind, or the way the water hits this boat, or it's the fucking oil monster of World War II, I have no idea. But whatever it is, it isn't going to make you feel any better about yourself or help you understand how all the bad stuff happened. So get the hell down here and be in your life. Be with me."

Abruptly, Harry smiled. His familiar, seven-year-old, wheedling smile.

"I'll be one second," he said. "Don't wait."

"I won't," I said. And I didn't.

4

Four hours later, pacing the beach with the echoes of the current still drumming in my skin like aftershocks, I watched the police I'd called on the cell phone I'd found in the glove box of the truck troll the area around the ship and beyond it in their patrol boats. A rescue team went on board, too, and stayed there for hours, but they didn't find or hear anything. They asked what we'd been doing out there, and I said exploring, and they shook their heads. They asked what I thought had happened to my cousin, and I said I thought he'd drowned, which seemed reasonable to me.

The water had been horrific on the way back, much harsher than coming out, and there'd been one awful moment, fish and turtles scattering all over the reef as though something huge and hungry and terrifying was coming, but nothing did.

Later, huddled under a police blanket at the little Lanai airport terminal, waiting for the next plane to the mainland, I called my mother and told her Harry had killed himself.

I think I made myself believe that for years. Long enough to get through college, start to build a mainland life for myself, then call Lanai information one day from my little Sacramento efficiency, get the number for Marion Jones, grade-school principal, explain who I was, and ask for a job.

I've been here ever since, in my little green hut on the outskirts of Haole Camp. The island children like me, mostly, because I teach them karate after math and have Gameboys in my room for them to play with. Marion likes me because I show up for work every day and don't drink and don't smile much. Some evenings, especially in the summer, when there isn't work even Marion can think of doing, she comes to my hut, and we barbecue chicken and onions and pineapples, and after dinner, we take a drive up to the Garden of the Gods and prowl separately through those giant stones, among the axis deer and wild horses, until the sun goes down.

Every Sunday, regular as church, I make my way to Shipwreck Beach, and I spread a tarp across the driftwood, and I watch the ship ride its reef to forever and make no sound whatsoever. The sound has gone. Marion thinks my doing this is a little unhealthy. It's the only thing she's ever reprimanded me for. She tells me my cousin jumped, forfeited his life, and deserves my pity but not so much of my time.

I have never tried to explain—to her, or anyone—that my cousin didn't jump. Couldn't have. It wasn't in his nature, though I didn't realize it until too late, right as I got that last, sun-blind glimpse of his face. I should have known it before, aboard the ship. *"I didn't do it for me,"* he'd said, and of course, as usual, in his way, he was telling the truth. Whatever the mechanism is that keeps our consciences from devouring us from within, like acid reflux, Harry's was still working. Maybe too well. He didn't want to die. He never had. He wanted to be better than he was, and he wanted not to have done the things he'd done. Like most of us.

And he wanted one more thing, and that was what caused him to wreak such havoc all his life, and was also the reason I loved him. He wanted—desperately, hopelessly—to make whoever was around him happy, at all times. He bought Randy Lynne beer because Randy Lynne wanted it. He told my mother he loved her because he thought my mother needed to hear it. He told me he was alright because he knew I'd come for reassurance. He killed the moth in Puhi's Den to keep it from tormenting Teddy the Lava King. And he opened the hold on that marooned ship because he thought there was something locked inside it that wanted out.

My mother has come to Lanai only once. She skulked around the island for five days, built me two bookshelves to get some of the piles off the floor, bought me an open plane ticket to return to the mainland, and left. "You're punishing yourself for nothing," she told me in the Garden of the Gods on her last night. "He was nothing. He was a bastard. He was never worth it. You're too smart, Amelia, too powerful a person to drown in Harry's whirlpool. The fact is, people go where they want to go. Remember that."

She may be right. Probably, she is. But I keep seeing Harry weeping on the deck of the ship, keep feeling his shoulder blades convulsing under my fingers like beating wings: my cousin, who broke my aunt's heart and embittered my mother and caused a stranger's death and loved me more than anyone else has or can or will. And I say we go where our ghosts lead us, drawn down the years like water across a continent. We have no choice, and there are no escape routes. But maybe—if we can just get ourselves still enough, our regrets quiet enough, our breathing steady and our ears and eyes wide open—maybe we can see the sea before we join it.

Mr. Dark's
Carnival

"The Montanan
is both humbled
and exalted by
this blazing glory
filling his world,
yet so quickly dead."

—JOSEPH KINSEY HOWARD,
MONTANA-HIGH, WIDE AND HANDSOME

So the first question, really," I said, leaning on my lectern and looking over the heads of my students at the twilight creeping off the plains into campus, "is, does anyone know anyone who has actually been there?"

Hands went up instantly, as they always do. For a few moments, I let the hands hang in the air, start to wilt under the fluorescent light, while I watched the seniors on the roof of Powell House dorm across the quad drape the traditional black bunting down the side of the building, covering all the windows. By the time I got outside, I knew, there would be straw corpses strewn all over campus and papier-mâché skeletons swinging in the trees. Few, if any, of the students who hung them there would have any cognizance of the decidedly sinister historical resonance of their actions.

"Right," I said, and returned my attention to my freshman seminar on eastern Montana history. It was the one undergraduate class I still taught each year. It was the one class I would never give up. "Primary-source accounts only, please."

"Meaning stuff written at the time?" said the perpetually confused Robert Hayright from the front row.

"That is indeed one correct definition of a primary source, Mr. Hayright. But in this case, I mean only interviews you have conducted or overheard yourself. No stories about third parties."

Two-thirds of the hands drooped to their respective desktops.

"Right. Let's eliminate parents and grandparents, now, who, over the centuries, have summoned and employed all sorts of bogeymen to keep their children careful as they exit the safeties of home."

Most of the rest of the hands went down.

"High-school chums, of course, because the whole game in high school, especially Eastern Montana high school, is to have been somewhere your classmates haven't, isn't it? To have seen and known the world?"

"I have a question, Professor R." said Tricia Corwyn from the front row, crossing her stockinged legs under her silky skirt and pursing her too-red mouth. Around her, helpless freshman boys squirmed in their seats. The note of flirtation in her tone wasn't for me, I knew. It was a habit, quite possibly permanent, and it made me sad. It has taken most of a century to excise most of the rote machismo from Montana's sons. Maybe next century, we can go to work on the scars that machismo has left on its daughters.

"If we eliminate secondhand accounts, parents, and high-school friends, who's left who could tell us about it?"

"My dear," I said, "you have the makings of a historian. That's a terrific question."

I watched Tricia trot out that string of studiously whitened teeth like a row of groomed show-horses, and abruptly I stood up straight, allowing myself a single internal head-shake. *My dear*. The most paternalistic and subtle weapon of diminishment in the Montana teacher's arsenal.

Pushing off the lectern and standing up straight, I said, "In fact, that's so good a question that I'm going to dodge it for the time being." A few members of the class were still alert or polite enough to smile. I saw the astonishing white hair of Robin Mills, the Humanities Department secretary, form in the doorway of my classroom like a cumulus cloud, but I ignored her for the time being. "Let me ask this. How many of you know anyone— once again, primary sources only, please—who claims to have worked there?"

This time, a single hand went up. That's one more than I'd ever had go up before.

"Mr. Hayright?" I said.

"My dog," he said, and the class exploded into laughter. But Robert Hayright continued. "It's true."

"Your dog told you this?"

"My dog Droopy disappeared on Halloween night three years ago. The next morning, a neighbor brought him home and told my dad a man in a clown suit had brought her to their door at six in the morning and said, 'Thank you for the dog, he's been at Mr. Dark's.'"

Mr. Hayright's classmates erupted again, but I didn't join them. The clown suit was interesting, I thought. A completely new addition to the myth.

"So let's see," I said gently. "Counting your father, your neighbor, and the clown"—this brought on more laughter, though I was not mocking—"your story is, at best, thirdhand."

"Not counting the dog," said Robert Hayright, and he grinned, too. At least this time, I noted, everyone seemed to be laughing with him.

In the doorway, Robin Mills cleared her throat, and her mass of white hair rippled. "Professor Roemer?"

"Surely this can wait, Ms. Mills," I said.

"Professor, it's Brian Tidrow."

I scowled. I couldn't help it. "Whatever he's got can definitely wait."

Instead of speaking, Robin Mills mouthed the rest. She did it three times, although I understood her the second time.

"That fucker," I muttered, but not quietly enough, and my students stopped laughing and stared. I ignored them. "Does Kate know?" I asked Robin.

"No one's seen her yet."

"Find her. Find her now. Tell her I'll be there soon."

For a second, Robin lingered in the doorway. I don't know if she expected comfort or company or just more reaction, but I wasn't planning on giving her any. Brian Tidrow was a descendant of a Crow who'd married a white woman and scouted for and died with Custer. He was also a third-generation alcoholic, arguably the brightest graduate student I'd ever taught, and almost certainly the one I had enjoyed least. Now, he had finally committed the supreme act of havoc wreaking he'd been threatening for years. He would get no more reaction from me, ever. I glared at Robin until she ducked her head and turned from the door.

"What was that about, Professor R.?" Tricia asked.

I avoided thinking about Kate. About Kate and Brian. What was there to think about? It had been years ago. By the time Robin located her for me, class would be over, and I'd be on my way. "You will notice, my young scholars, that I didn't even ask if any of you have been there. I have lived in Clarkston all my life, except for my eight years of university and graduate work. My parents lived here all their lives. My grandparents came from Germany right before the First World War"—*at least several hundred years after my father, and half a century after my mother,'* as Brian Tidrow loved to remind me—"and never left until their deaths. In all that time, not a single member of my family has ever encountered anyone who has actually, personally, been. Ever. And that leads us to the most alarming, the most discomfiting question of all. Is it possible that Mr. Dark's Carnival—the inspiration for all our Halloween festivities, the most celebrated attraction or event in the history of Clarkston, Montana—never really existed?"

As always, that question took just a moment to land. It floated through the room for a few seconds like an Alka-Seltzer tablet dropped into a glass. And then it began to fizz.

"Wait," said one of the boys near Tricia.

"Oh my God, no way," said Tricia, her blue eyes bright as they blazed through boy after boy.

Robert Hayright shook his head. "That's wrong. You're wrong, Professor. I know it."

I put my hand up, but the fizzing continued a while longer. When it quieted at last, I started to smile, thought of Brian Tidrow with his great-grandfather's Winchester rifle gripped in his teeth, and shuddered. *Goddamn him,* I thought. I refused to offer him any additional respect simply because he'd finally had the stupidity—he'd probably have called it guts—to go and do it.

"What do you know, Mr. Hayright?"

"I know there was a Carnival in 1926. It was out in the fallow fields by where the Gulf station at the edge of town is now."

"How do you know that?"

"We studied it in high school. There were newspaper reports. Primary sources." He glanced up at me to see if I'd stop him, then went on. "Livestock that vanished. Some guy in a black robe seen drifting around on the prairie and lurking in the bushes. Three people died of fright, including a policemen sent to investigate all the screaming."

"There was another in 1943," I said quietly, to the suddenly silent room, as the icy twilight permeated the windows and seeped into the corners like floodwater. "That one was in particularly poor taste. Reportedly, it was haunted by dozens of people outfitted as dead soldiers. Upset a lot of parents whose sons were currently overseas.

"In 1978, there were no less than three so-called Mr. Dark's Carnivals rumored around town, though two of them were meant for small children and the third turned out to be a dance. I'm not saying no one has ever called their haunted house 'Mr. Dark's Carnival.' But as to the existence of the legendary, mystery-shrouded Carnival-to-end-all-Carnivals. . . ." I waved my hand, started to smile, sighed instead. "The fact is that every year, we build our haunted houses and collect our children and head out to cover as much of our fair miniature city as we can, hoping for that supreme horrifying experience. That haunted house that will detonate our bowels, grind our chattering teeth to rubble, and blast us out the other side shaken and giggling and alive. That Mr. Dark's Carnival that we've been told, all our lives, might just be out there, on some unnamed street, in some unexpected and unexplored corner."

For the next fifteen minutes, students hurled questions about the most persistent and ubiquitous elements of the myth—the tickets that had to be given to you or found somewhere, the ever-changing locations, the reputed deaths by fright. Most years, I let this part of the discussion go as long as it would, because I enjoyed hearing the variations on the legend, and the students enjoyed having the legend exploded. But this year, feeling increasingly disturbed that Robin had not floated back into the door to say she'd found Kate, and unable to shake the picture I'd formed of Brian Tidrow's last moments on Earth, I ticked off my myth-destroying points in mere minutes.

How many unexplored corners were there, exactly, in a town barely eleven miles square and 145 years old? How many new locations could there be? If tickets had to be found or given, who did the hiding and giving? Given the elaborate nature of the illusions attributed to Mr. Dark's, where were all the workers necessary to perpetuate them?

Finally, Tricia once again asked the most significant remaining question. "Was there even a Mr. Dark?"

"Oh yes," I said, even more quietly, and the class hushed once more. "Although as to why this story has attached himself to him, well—"

It was at that moment, of course, that Robin Mills finally returned. How not surprising, I thought, indulging just a little selfish fury, that Brian Tidrow's farewell gesture should destroy my favorite moment of the teaching year. The only thing that even came close was the day I marched into my graduate seminar, laid a map detailing the progress of cattle introduction onto the open range over another showing the path of buffalo depletion, and proved, or at least suggested, that despite all our best efforts and a hundred years of imprecise historical accounting, it was anthrax, not white men—not directly, anyway—that killed the buffalo.

Outside, gray lines of snow began to drag themselves over the ground like the fringe on a giant, smothering carpet. The clouds hung heavy and low, and the first unmistakable winter wind gnawed and whined at the windows. I thought of Kate, and forgot about anger, forgot about my teaching and my love for Halloween. I started to ache.

"Scholars, I apologize," I said. "There has been a personal crisis in the Humanities Department, and I need to tend to it immediately. So we will have to continue this discussion on Monday."

"What about Mr. Dark?" Robert Hayright whined, sounding almost angry. I didn't blame him. My class had been the most popular freshman elective for most of a decade, primarily because of the lecture I gave each year on this date.

I began to slide the notes I never used into my backpack, watched Robert Hayright slouch in his seat while Tricia rose in front of him. "Who knows?" I said, catching Robin Mills's agitated tapping against the door frame of my room with a pen. "Perhaps one of you will find a strip of paper tacked to a tree trunk tonight, and stare at it in disbelief. And you'll find the real Mr. Dark. And on Monday, you'll be able to tell me just how wrong I've been all these years. All right, I see you, Ms. Mills."

"Sorry, Professor," I heard her say. "Didn't even know what I was doing."

"Have a recommendation?" Tricia asked as the class began to file out. She was leaning forward over my desk, too close to me. Habit, again.

"About what, Ms. Corwyn?" I continued putting away papers but avoided brushing her sweater with my arm.

"Haunted houses we shouldn't miss? Particularly good streets? I hear they're going to have monsters in the river."

Startled, I looked up and found myself submerged in those too-blue eyes. "No one's done that for years," I said, and the last of my anger sank into sadness, though none of it was for Brian Tidrow. Other people have Christmases or High Holidays, and families to share them with. I have Halloween, and these kids. This year, I would have neither. "You'll have to tell me about it."

"I will," she said. "Thanks for the great class."

Seconds later, they were gone, and all the energy in the room went with them, and I was just another academia ghost, my skin sporting that translucent, sickly fluorescent tan, my hair succumbing to the color-leaching chalk dust and dead air. I wanted to see Kate. I wanted to help her fight through this. For the first time in my life, I wanted Halloween to be over.

"Where is she?" I said to Robin Mills.

"Your place," she said, with no trace of the contempt she might otherwise have attached to that statement. "She called from there. She was apparently the one who found him, Professor."

"Goddamn Brian," I said. "Goddamn him to hell." I started past Robin. I saw her start to register shock, because that's the emotion recommended, I guess, in the Judgmental and Officious Department Secretary Handbook for such comments and situations.

But then she said, "Tell Kate we're all thinking of her. Tell her to come see me Monday, or whenever she wants."

I turned, smiled, and realized that I'd worked near, if not

exactly with, this person for fourteen years, and that it was time I got over myself. "I will," I said. "Thanks."

Seconds later, I was strolling through the deepening dark across campus. In the trees, paper men danced and spun on the frigid wind. I heard whooping sounds from the row of fraternity houses at the campus's south end, and scurrying feet as students raced excitedly for their assigned posts in haunted houses or collected dates for the evening tour through town. Underneath it all, I heard the ceaseless, sucking emptiness of the prairie, slowly pulling this town piece by piece and person by person back into the sea of cheatgrass and oblivion.

By the time I turned onto Winslow Street and left campus, the cold had crawled inside my insufficient fall windbreaker, and I could feel it creeping down my bones toward the dead center of me. The little kids were out already, racing down sidewalks lined with lit pumpkins in paper bags that glowed a glorious, leering orange. I saw a green-skinned zombie shiver up from a pile of dead leaves in the corner of a lawn and grab for two bewinged little girls who giggled and fled. The zombie watched them and smiled and shivered backwards and drew the leaves over himself again. He would be there all evening, I knew. He would keep his smile to himself for longer when the older kids came, grab a little more forcefully. He'd be frozen half through when he got home, and full of civic pride. In some towns, the neighbors force you to keep your yard tidy. In others, you're expected to show up in church, or help out at the food bank or on Clean the River Beaches Day. In Clarkston, you participate in Halloween.

A half mile from campus, the houses spread out onto their lots, and the paths marked by the paper-bag pumpkins disappeared. But the festivities continued. Even the country club haunted its golf course every year and opened it to the entire town, though they taped tarpaulins down on the putting greens. At this hour, though, with full dark not yet fallen, these streets were relatively silent. The scares out here, it was understood, were for older kids. The zombies in the leaf piles sometimes held on to you if they caught you. I stopped just a moment outside Dean Harry Piltner's house and stood in the strings of snow. As usual, Harry had constructed a long, knee-high crawl-through maze of straw that zigzagged back and forth across his yard. I'd once asked him where he got the wolf spiders and finger-sized roaches he occasionally set free in there to scurry and hunt and, usually, die by squishing at the hands of some screaming teen. He just smiled in response and kept his Halloween secret to himself, like any good Clarkstonian. The homemade brownies his wife left at the exit of the maze were the best anyone I knew had ever tasted.

The Blackroot River bisects Clarkston five different times as it bends back and forth through town, creating miniature peninsulas. My house, a turn-of-the-century A-frame built by one of the railroad masterminds of the Land Grab that brought homesteaders to the open range and, very nearly, civil war to the plains, rides the point of Purviston, the town's easternmost peninsula, like the smokestack on a steam train. As I crossed the footbridge that leads directly to my door, I scanned my house for lights but saw none. Either Kate had left, or she was sitting in the dark. I suspected the latter. In moments of personal and professional crisis, Kate clung to the shadows. Otherwise, she'd never have let Brian lure her to Montana for her graduate work, leaving offers from four Ivies in her wake.

For just a moment, in the center of the bridge, I stopped to listen to the river. Already, its gurgle had an ugly rasp. By Thanksgiving, it would be frozen, and the streets would tuck themselves into their winter hibernation under a thick blanket of snow. I glanced back toward town, saw orange lights winking through the dark and heard a small child's scream erupt in the air like the call of a hunting osprey.

"You missed all the good stuff, Brian," I mumbled, surprising myself. I hadn't known I was thinking of him.

Even after I unlocked the door, it took me a few seconds to realize Kate was there, hunched on the couch by the bay window overlooking the river. She had the blue blanket my mother had knitted me, years and years ago, wrapped around her waist, and her long brown hair draped on her shoulders like a shawl. In sunlight, Kate's oddly sunken brown eyes made her look as though she never quite got enough sleep. In the half-light, the shadows lent color to her wan skin, and her eyes seemed to creep forward, and she became an astonishingly beautiful woman. At least, she became one to me.

"Hey," I said, started toward her, and felt just a flicker of the old uncertainty. I've long since gotten over my guilt about dating Kate; though she is a former graduate student of mine, she's thirty-five, all of six years younger, with more of an academic pedigree than I ever had and no reason whatsoever to let me exploit her, or to exploit me. But I was eleven years without a significant relationship before Kate—Clarkston is a tiny, tiny place, the university tinier still, and I was born reticent, anyway—and even after two years, I've yet to regain my confidence completely.

This night, Kate did nothing to make it easy for me. She stared out the window. The window was closed, but the snow seemed to have seeped into the room somehow. I imagined I could see it winking near her ears like a cloud of will-o'-the-wisps, about to spirit her away. Stepping to the couch, I dropped down beside her. She started to cry quietly. I sat and held her hand and let her.

"He wasn't even a good friend," Kate murmured, after a long, long while. "He wasn't ever."

I touched her hair. "No, he wasn't."

"Too unreliable. Too wrapped up in his own pathetic problems."

"He was sick, Kate. He didn't have a choice."

For the first time that night, she turned and looked at me. The depth of her eye sockets made it seem as if I was peering into a cave. The effect always made me want to crawl in there with her. She smiled, and I felt like laughing but didn't.

"This is a reversal," she said.

"Don't get me wrong, Kate-O. I wish he'd never come back here—except for the bringing you with him part. I wish you'd never known him. You or anyone else in the damn department, because he had that mopey, haunted intensity that all you grad students flock to like bees to pollen, and then you spread it, and then everybody's mopey and haunted."

Kate laughed, and this time, the laugh inside me slipped out.

"He was a good historian," she said, returning the squeeze of my hand now.

"He was a promising historian. *You're* a good one. You do the research first, then have your insights."

Without warning, she was crying again, whether for Brian Tidrow or her mother, also dead by suicide more than twenty years before, or her vindictive father, or something else entirely, I didn't know.

This time, the crying spell lasted over an hour. I listened to her breath sputter and her voice murmur and choke, watched Halloween night settle over Clarkston. The snow thickened, gathering itself on the dead grass and in the cracks on the pavement. Even through the closed windows, shouts and screams and bursts of organ music reached us from across the river. "I stepped in some of his hair," Kate mumbled at one point, and I winced and squeezed her hand as she shook. I'd forgotten she'd found him.

It was at least eight and maybe later when Kate looked up

at me. The shaking in her shoulders had stilled just a little. But what she said was, "This could go on all night, David. You should go."

I blinked, startled, not sure how to answer. "Go where? This is my home. And also where I want to be."

"It's Halloween. The best day of your life, remember?"

The sentimental response proved irresistible. I hadn't had many opportunities to try one, after all. "I've had other best days, lately," I said. Then I blushed, grinning like a six-year-old, and Kate burst out laughing.

"Go haunted-housing. Come back with stories."

"Come with me."

Instantly, her smile vanished. "I've seen my dead person for the day, thanks. Oh, fuck, David." Her face crumpled again. I reached for her hand, but she shook it off. "Really," she snapped, and I jerked back. "I want you to go. I want to be alone."

"Kate, I want to be with you."

"You *are* with me," she said, still snapping.

For a long moment, we stared at each other. Then I picked my coat off the chair where I'd draped it and stood. I started to ask if she was sure, but she was. And quite frankly, I was relieved, in all sorts of ways. I knew that I'd done what I could and that my actions had been noted. I knew that Kate loved me. And I knew that I wasn't going to miss Halloween after all.

"I'll bring you back a brownie," I said.

"God, you're not going to crawl through Piltner's maze, are you?"

I just stood there.

"You're an eight-year-old, David."

"I'll check back in an hour. I won't be gone long."

"All right," Kate said, but she was already withdrawing into her crouch with her gaze aimed out the window.

I opened the front door, stepped outside, and the cold jumped me. It had teeth and claws, and the way it tore at my skin had me checking my coat front for rips. "Jesus," I said, started to turn back inside for gloves and scarf, and thought better of it. I didn't want to be gone long, anyway. And I didn't want to disturb Kate now. Shoving my hands in my pockets and blinking my watering eyes, I drove forward into the dark. Because I had my head down, I didn't see the thing on the footbridge until I was almost on top of it. Gasping, I jerked to a stop.

At first, all I saw was a newspaper blown open. Then the wind kicked up, and the edges lifted like wings but the paper itself stayed put, and I realized there was something underneath it holding it in place. A half step closer, and I thought I could see a head-shaped shadow lying in the larger, deeper shadow of the overhanging poplar trees like . . . well, like a head in a pool of blood.

Goddamn Brian Tidrow, I thought again, and started forward. The man lay straight across the bridge, in the dead center of it, with his head against one railing and his feet dangling over the river on the far side. I've often wondered where all the homeless people in Clarkston come from, and why they stay. I never recognize any of them—they're no one I ever knew—despite my years of living here. And the climate can't be conducive to life on the street. Maybe the citizenry are generous, or the food at the shelters is good, or else the plains loom like the roiling oceans of nothing they are and obliterate hopes of safe passage.

This man, I decided, was sleeping or stone drunk. You'd have to be drunk to sleep in this spot, with the wind crawling over you. The only movement as I approached was the fluttering of the newspaper. The only sounds came from the river below and the town beyond.

"Hey, man," I said softly. "You all right?"

The newspaper fluttered. The river hissed. The man lay still.

I thought about going home to call the police. I had nothing against the poor guy sleeping on my bridge, but jail would be warmer. Kate wanted me gone, though. And sometimes, I thought, with the fatuous logic of the comfortable, there are better things to be than warm. I planted one foot, lifted the other so that I was straddling the man, and he sat up.

It was the hand he snarled in the belt of my coat, I think, that kept me from leaping straight over the railing. Clumps of curly black hair flew from his scalp like strips of shredded steel wool. His lips were white blue with cold, his eyes so bloodshot that the red seemed to have overrun the irises and pooled in the pupils.

For a few seconds, he held me there, and I held my breath, and nothing moved. He wasn't looking at me but beyond me, past my hip at the trees and the riverbank. The intensity of his stare made me want to whirl around, but I couldn't rip my gaze from his face.

Finally, I managed to gulp some air into my lungs, and the cold shocked them out of paralysis. I coughed. The man gripped my coat, stared behind me, and said nothing.

"What?" I finally said.

The hand at my waist did not relax. The direction of the gaze didn't change.

"Are you cold? Can I—" I looked down and saw the crumple of black paper pressed between the man's palm and my stomach. A whole new shudder rippled through me, drawn from a long-forgotten childhood reservoir. Blind Pew, and the Black Spot, and the Admiral Benbow Inn. *Until dark*, Pew told Billy Bones, on the day of Billy Bones's death. *They'll come at dark.*

I put my hand on the paper, which turned out to be surprisingly heavy. Construction paper. Instantly, the homeless man's hand ricocheted back to his side as though I'd triggered a cata-pult. The whole body beneath me jerked backward into a prone position, and the newspaper snapped into place around him. Uncrumpling the construction paper, still shuddering, I stepped back and looked at what I'd been given.

"Oh," I said. Then I said it again. Then I turned and raced for home.

Kate was still crouched by the window when I burst in. She didn't look up to ask what I'd forgotten. She looked only a little more conscious than the man on the bridge had. I marched straight to her anyway.

"Look," I said, and held the construction paper toward her. "Kate, I'm serious. Look."

Her sigh came from way down inside her. Slowly, she took the paper from me, tilted it toward the light coming in the window. She read it twice. Then she stood up. The blanket stayed wrapped around her waist.

"God, David, we have to go," she said. "I'll get my coat."

"I'm going to marry this woman," I said aloud to the window as Kate stepped toward the closet. By the time she returned to me, buttoning her heaviest black overcoat around her, her movements had regained most of their usual speed and grace.

"You have to understand," I told her, touching her hair with the back of my hand. Her face still looked wan, but her eyes were bright. "This won't be my first Mr. Dark's Carnival."

"What do you mean? You don't even believe it's real."

"I've been given tickets on three previous occasions. Twice, I followed the directions on them and wound up at a frat party. Little Halloween prank from my students. The third time, I wound up at a very fine haunted house indeed, right here in Purviston, not five hundred feet from this door. Unfortunately, I happened to recognize Harry Piltner's stoop under his black cowl at the doorway, and because I'm a jerk, I said, 'Do I get a brownie, Har?' And Harry kicked me."

"So why are we going?" Kate said, shepherding me toward the door.

"Get gloves. Hat, too. It's unbelievably cold."

We were outside now, and Kate threw her head back and stood a moment in the chill. She didn't even have her coat buttoned all the way.

"You're insane," I said, jamming my gloved hands into my pockets and hunching against the snap of the wind. "We're going, first of all, because someone went to a lot of trouble to get me these. Get somebody these, anyway. And they did it with high Clarkston Halloween style, so I can't ignore it. Secondly, even if it's a frat party, the beer'll be good."

"Oh, right. You don't even drink."

I held the door of my rusty red 1986 Volvo open for her, kissed the top of her head as she bent to climb in. "You're freezing," I said. "Put on your damn hat."

"Thirdly?" she said, and smiled up at me. At that moment, she seemed even more excited than I had to admit I was.

"Thirdly, I had a feeling you'd come, in spite of everything."

Her smile widened.

"And fourthly, Kate dear." I glanced toward the bridge, which was empty. Purviston tickets distributed, I thought. I wondered where the homeless man would lay himself and his newspaper next. "Fourthly, one just never knows, does one? I don't, anyway." I shut her door and got in on my side.

The car took four cranks of the ignition key, but it did start. It always starts. "Where to?" I said, gesturing toward the black construction paper in Kate's lap. On it, in gray white chalk, was a map of Clarkston with a white dotted line snaking through it and the words *Mr. Dark's Carnival Welcomes You* underneath. No skull and crossbones this time, and no come-if-you-dare warning. A classier prank, at the very least, I thought.

"Get to Winslow," Kate said, without looking down at the paper. "Take it south all the way out of town."

To my relief, she sounded excited. Exhausted, wrecked, but excited. I threw the car's heater on, blasting us both with frigid air, and grunted. Kate stared out the window at the dark.

By now, even the streets of Purviston were alive with costumed revelers. A group of rubber-masked teens came hurtling down the sidewalk from the direction of Harry Piltner's, their wigs and winter coats caked with straw, hands flashing all over themselves in search of bugs that had probably long since dropped off. I smiled.

In town, the activity level seemed just slightly lower than usual because of the cold. By 9:30, most Halloweens, the college kids who worked the little-kid haunted houses had been released from scare duty, and they clustered around parked cars or outside the Rangehand pub downtown and blasted hip-hop and waited for midnight, when the frat parties began in earnest and continued until the police shut them down. But this night, the trick-or-treaters had long since retreated indoors, and the partiers had stayed in their dorms, and the only people out were the heartiest Clarkstonians, tracing their habitual routes from one fright sight to the next.

In a matter of minutes, we were out of town. At the two-mile mark, the last streetlamp stuck out of the prairie like a flag left by a lunar expedition, and then we were in darkness.

"Still know where we're going?" I said.

"Says seven miles."

"Air's getting warm."

Kate didn't answer. Snow glittered on the asphalt and the endless stunted grass all around us, as though the sky itself had shattered on the ground. The eastern Montana plains on a snowlit night are limitless as deep space and just as empty.

After a minute or so, Kate shifted in her seat. She spoke slowly, softly. She sounded barely awake, and most likely she was after the day she'd had, and now the warming car, the chattering road, the silence. "Tell me again what you think you know, David Roemer, about Albert Aloysius Dark?"

Instantly, the last of my classroom lecture leapt to my lips. "Delighted you asked. Thought I wasn't going to get to tell anyone this year."

Kate smiled.

"Judge Albert Aloysius Dark. Born God-knows-where, educated God-knows-where, because that's the first intriguing thing about him, isn't it? There's no record of him in this state—it was a territory then, of course—before his appointment to the Bench in September, 1877. In fact, there's no record of him anywhere."

"You mean you haven't found records of him yet."

"You're not the only competent researcher in this Volvo, O Barely Speaking Woman. And I'll thank you to remember the Civil War, and its prodigious though little-noted effects on the record keeping of our fair cities and towns."

Kate nodded. "Go on."

"For eight years after his appointment as ranking judge in this desolate region, Judge Dark maintained a consistently moderate record. Right up until Christmas Eve, 1885. That ni—"

"Turn here," Kate said, and I jammed on the brakes, dragged the car to a stop, and stared.

"Turn where?"

"Back up."

I looked over my shoulder into the black, snow-streaked nothing. "Maybe the map's upside down."

Kate grinned. "Just back up, idiot."

I tapped the brake pedal, held it down so that my taillights illuminated the blackness. There, fifteen feet or so behind the car, limned in red paint of some sort, were two tire ruts snaking between two bedraggled plains shrubs and away into the grass. Way down in my stomach, something twitched. Nervousness. Uneasiness, maybe. Disbelief. Hope. If this was a prank, or an imitation, it was the best yet. And if it wasn't a prank . . .

"How the hell did you know that was there?"

"The map."

"But how did you see it?"

"I was looking for it. David, let's go." Kate looked at me. Her face was still red, but whether from crying or excitement, I couldn't tell.

Backing us up, I paused just a moment at the lip of the path. I cracked my window, and the whistling silence sucked at our little bubble of life inside the car.

"What are you thinking?" Kate said softly.

"Little Big Horn. The Donner Party. Fifteen or twenty other examples of overconfident white people overestimating their power over the West."

"This really could be it, David. Couldn't it?"

"It really could be something."

I pushed my foot on the gas, and we were off the highway, jiggling over the dirt.

"How far?" I mumbled.

Kate glanced down at the map. "Three miles, maybe." I groaned. Kate said, "Christmas Eve, 1885."

I watched the grass disappear under our tires, the snow that seemed to float on ground so flat and featureless that it didn't even really seem to be there. "On Christmas Eve, 1885, at approximately 8:45 P.M., a group of local ranchers calling themselves the Guardians of Right appeared at the door of Judge Dark's rather lavish creekside home—it was destroyed by fire, incidentally in 1956, and is now buried under the high-school football stadium—and demanded entrance. With them, the Guardians had brought a Chinese homesteader who'd been hitched to a wagon with his feet bound and made to hop all the way from his claim two miles outside of town."

"How do we know this?" Kate asked.

"Primary source, of course, of course. And no one can talk to a source, of course."

An old, habitual joke of mine. Kate ignored it. I went on.

"The judge himself kept an impressively detailed notebook. The Guardians demanded immediate entry, a trial right then and there, and a hanging verdict. And Judge Dark, inexplicably, showed the men into his living room, then called his wife down to act as court reporter and witness. The prosecution case lasted ten minutes, and involved somewhat circumstantial but undeniably incriminating evidence of the theft of foodstores and two horses. There was no defense, seeing as how the homesteader in question did not speak English and couldn't even stand because the bones in his feet and ankles had been smashed during his trip to the Judge's door. The guilty verdict and death sentence apparently came so fast that even the Guardians were startled into silence. The Judge makes specific and rather self-satisfied note of this effect.

"What the Judge actually said next, I cannot tell you. But I can tell you what he wrote. And I can tell you that word for word: *'I attached a single condition: that the prisoner be hanged by no hand but my own, and that he stay this night, his last on this Earth, in my home, under my care.'* This was assented to, and the stunned Guardians left. And on Christmas morning, in front of over a hundred witnesses in what was then the town square,

Judge Albert Dark wheeled the homesteader to a poplar tree, strung a rope around his neck, positioned him in a sort of crouch in the back of a wagon, and executed him, cleanly and quickly. No one yelled '3-7-77.'"

"What does that mean, by the way?"

"No one knows, really," I said. "None of the original Virginia City vigilantes ever said. They just left those numbers pinned to their victims. Anyway, the homesteader, by every account, said not a word, and made no sound. But he did look up, right as the wagon fled him and the rope bit into his neck. Two of the four published accounts claim he was smiling. Kate, what the hell is that?" But I could tell what it was. It was a kid. In pajamas.

He was barefoot in the grass, straddling the tire ruts with one arm stretched perfectly perpendicular to his shoulders, pointing off into the blackness. His skin glowed white in the headlight beams, as though the snow had somehow sunk inside it. He had short blond hair that stuck straight up. His pajamas had zebras on them.

I hit the brakes, started to slow.

"God," Kate said, as we rolled to a stop fifteen feet from the kid. "How old do you think he is?"

"How cold do you think he is?" I muttered, staring at the kid's feet.

He was about as tall as the top of my windshield. I rolled down my window and leaned out, but the child made no move toward the car, and he didn't lower his arm. It occurred to me that maybe he was an astoundingly realistic scarecrow. But he wasn't. I could see his lips, blue with cold, twitching when the prairie wind whipped across them.

"Are you all right?" I called. The child didn't move.

Then, abruptly, I smiled. I hadn't even gotten to this latest Mr.

Dark's Carnival, and already, it had me pleading with the ghouls, trying to get them to break and speak to me. The bubble of nervous excitement inside me swelled.

"Follow the yellow brick road," I said, and turned in the direction the child had pointed.

There were other tire tracks, I noted, all around us. I took an absurd amount of comfort in the fact that we weren't the first ones out here. I drove slowly, letting the prairie drum against the underside of the car like a choppy sea against the hull of a sailboat. Except for the dirt we stirred, nothing moved.

"How many did Judge Dark hang?" Kate asked, though her eyes, too, were straining forward into the void.

"Four, that we know of, between 1885 and statehood, when he drops from the official record as abruptly as he appeared. In each case, he allowed a local vigilante group to bring suspects to a lightning trial, convicted the suspects, then kept them all night in his home, where one assumes he served as confessor and last-meal chef or possibly something completely different, and then performed the killing the next morning. He apparently was a master executioner, because, according to the *Plains-Ledger*, *'not a single one of his charges so much as danced. And none of them said a word before they went to their makers.'*"

"Look," said Kate, but I'd already seen.

Drawing the car forward, I pulled into a space between two pickup trucks and switched off the ignition. There were six other vehicles arrayed around us in a makeshift parking lot. Of the drivers and passengers, I saw no trace.

I looked at Kate. We listened to the snow tap the roof of the Volvo. Beyond the impromptu circle of cars, the prairie grass rolled in the raging wind.

"So remind me," Kate murmured. "How did this murderous judge, whoever he was, become part of the Carnival myth?"

"Can't remind you," I said. " 'Cause I never told you. 'Cause I don't know."

"And why 'Carnival'? Why not 'Scary House'?"

"Got me yet again."

Suddenly Kate was smiling once more, and the red in her lips spread up her cheeks, and I felt so grateful, so lucky that I wasn't even sure I could move. "Thank you for coming to get me," she said.

"Thank you for coming along, my love."

Kate blew me a kiss. She jerked the door handle down, still smiling, and—gently, as though easing into water—climbed into the night. I opened my own door and joined her. We stood at the hood of the car and stared around us.

There was no sound except the wind in the grass. No child in pajamas appeared to point us the right way. I jammed my hands into my pockets as the cold gnawed at my wrists.

"There," I said.

"I see it," said Kate.

It was just a glow, barely brighter than the moonlight on the snow all around us. Distances are hard enough to gauge on the plains in broad daylight. But given the limited visibility, I decided the glow couldn't be more than a half mile away, straight out from the highway into the grass. We started walking.

It was an illusion, of course, that the dark got darker as soon as we left the circle of cars. Nevertheless, I could feel the eastern Montana night sweep over our heads on its enormous wings. I could feel its weight up there, and its talons. I kept my head down and walked. Kate walked beside me, the sleeve of her coat brushing rhythmically, repeatedly, against my own. We'd gone maybe 300 yards when both of us looked up together and saw the house.

It loomed out of the prairie shadows, black in the moonlight, inexplicable as the monolith in *2001*. The glow we saw came from a lone floodlight buried in the grass and aimed at the white fence surrounding the structure. As we got closer, I saw that the building wasn't black but barn red, single-storied and rectangular and long. In the yard demarcated by the fence, people-shaped figures glided back and forth.

"If it was nothing else but this," I said, staring at the tableau before me, "I think I'd be satisfied."

"It's like something out of a painting," Kate said, and that stopped me. The chill that flooded my mouth seemed to have come from inside rather than out.

For a second, I couldn't place the source of my discomfort. I looked at the structure. I looked at the floating figures, just beginning to acquire distinct faces from this distance. I looked at the fence, and then I had it.

Because it wasn't a fence. And the scene didn't remind me of a painting, but of a photograph. The one on page 212 of the Montana history primer I'd penned, to be exact, that showed the stacks of jumbled buffalo skeletons piled on the plains during the years the federal government paid the most desperate or ghastly Montanans to shoot every bison they could find and export the bones downriver.

I started to speak, had to wet my lips, tried again. "There, um, been any recently reported mass murders of oxen in the vicinity?"

Kate turned, her brow furrowed. "What?"

"Take a good gander at that fence, Kate."

She did. Then she said, "Ooh. That can't be real."

"One hopes not. One hopes there is a large placard pasted over the entry reassuring us that No Animals Were Harmed or Mistreated During Creation of This Carnival. But one is disturbed."

"Come on," Kate said, and on we went.

Up close, the bones looked a little less real, if only because they were reassuringly clean. Somehow, I'd been expecting bits of gristle to be hanging from them like party streamers. The four figures gliding back and forth in the house's mock garden were all young women, and they all wore long white nightgowns that flowed down their forms like liquid moonlight. They were bare-armed, black-haired, and they might have been sisters. Certainly, they all had the same porcelain skin pallor, the same slightly upturned noses, the same half smiles on their red-black lips. I found the sight of them slightly disappointing. After everything that had come so far, this seemed too familiar a horror movie image, and something of a failure of imagination.

The mound of bones—up close, it was more hedge than fence—had one opening off to the right side of the house. Crouching beside the opening, staring straight past us at the eternity of nothing beyond, was another child. This one wore a green overcoat belted at the waist. He had jet black hair that made his skin look bleached of features, like a face in a photographic negative. He, too, was barefoot.

When Kate and I moved toward the opening in the bones, the child stood up and stepped in front of us. We waited for him to speak, but of course he didn't. He didn't move, either.

"Now what?" I finally said.

The nightgown wraiths weren't the only people in the yard, I could see now. There were other people with plain old Montana-pale skin and good winter jackets and gloves and scarves. Hauntees. Maybe eight of them, milling about.

Slowly, still looking beyond us—just like the man on the bridge, I realized, and wondered if this particular Mr. Dark ran an extended and brilliantly effective training program for his employees—the gatekeeper child raised his arm, palm upward, and held it toward us.

"Blood?" I muttered to Kate. "Cheez-Its? What does he want?"

After a long moment, Kate dipped her hand into her coat pocket and withdrew the black construction paper. "Ticket," she said happily.

"Oh, yeah. Wouldn't want any party crashers," I said, but I moved forward with Kate as she placed the folded paper in the child's hand.

"Brrr," she said as she touched him. "Honey, you're freezing."

"It's not so bad," said the child, and my mouth flew open and my knees locked. I'd gotten used to the lack of response.

Kate maintained her poise better than I did. She glanced at me, then back at the child. Then she nodded. "You're right. It isn't." Taking my glove in her hand, she drew me forward through the bone hedge into the yard.

We'd taken all of three steps when one of the winter coat-wrapped figures threw back the flaps of its red wool cap and squeaked, "Professor R!" at me.

I blinked, glanced at Kate, then back at the person flouncing toward me. "Um," I said. I run into students every time I leave my house in Clarkston. But somehow, for no good reason, I'd forgotten it was possible tonight. I blushed. "Hello, Ms. Corwyn."

"And who's this?" said Tricia, completely unaffected.

My blush deepened, and I felt a flicker of annoyance. Surely, at age forty-one, after seventeen years in the classroom, I'd stopped being embarrassed about the gaps that existed between my teaching self and my home self. But that didn't mean I'd found a way to bridge or even explain them. I don't know anyone who has. "This is Kate," I finally answered.

I turned to Kate for a smile, a gently mocking put-down, something. But the expression on her face had sagged. She looked at me, and she seemed so tired, all of a sudden, and I knew Brian Tidrow had floated up over her shoulder. He'd done that periodically, even when he was alive. It wouldn't be the last time, I knew.

"Okay," she said, and wandered away into the garden. I had no idea what she meant.

"Hmmm," said Tricia.

Instantly, with Kate out of earshot, I was Professor Roemer once more. "You just keep those fast-developing observational skills to yourself," I said, and smiled with my mouth closed. A teacherly smile.

"Is this unbelievable or what? This corpse crawled up out of the river and gave me a map."

"A corpse."

"All white. I don't even know how long he was down there, because I sure didn't see him. Robert and I were walking along the bank in Poplar Park and suddenly this *thing* wriggled up out of the water at our feet. He was stark naked except for a Speedo. Robert almost flew up the nearest tree."

I went right past the corpse. A Speedo-wearing corpse in a half-frozen river did not seem so very strange on a Clarkston Halloween night. At least, not this Clarkston Halloween night. "Robert," I said. "Robert Hayright?"

"Yeah," said Tricia. "Why?"

I felt my jaw start to drop, clamped it shut. Annoyance flared in me, though I had no idea why. I needed to go to Kate. And I wanted to get lost in the marvelous atmosphere of this haunted house. But I couldn't quite wade out of Tricia's blue eyes yet. And I couldn't get comfortable with the way she floated through the world. I'd met people like her before, of course. A few. The ones born with smarts, beauty, self-confidence, everything, gliding on their own private seas, remote and mesmerizing as lighted yachts as they drift among the teeming rest of us, struggling in our leaky johnboats from one shore we can't remember toward another we'll never know.

"How did that happen?" I said.

Tricia shrugged. "Robert? He asked."

Good for both of you, I almost said, then decided that was beyond condescending. "I have to go find Kate."

"Don't miss the booth. It's weird as hell. Professor R., do you think this is it? The real Mr. Dark's?"

I studied her cold-flushed, happy, markless face. And my annoyance transformed into sadness, still and deep. "I think it may be our Mr. Dark's, Tricia. I think this may be as close as we'll ever get." Not until I was several steps away did it occur to me to wonder where Robert Hayright was.

In the back left corner of the house's backyard sat a game booth draped in red and yellow carnival bunting. Kate stood to the left of it, but she wasn't playing whatever game the booth offered. She was looking at the prairie outside the bone hedge.

I was fifteen feet away, closing fast, when two of the night-gowned girls appeared on either side of Kate, took her arms, and spun her, gently, toward the house. I hurried forward.

"Wait," I called.

"Move it, come on," Kate answered, turning her head toward me but letting the nightgown girls lead her. The spirit of the evening seemed to have seized her once more. "I think it's our turn, David."

They were guiding her around the side of the structure toward the front door. Like all haunted houses, I surmised, Mr. Dark's could accommodate only a few guests at a time. Then the illusions had to be reset, the trapdoors and lunging scarecrow monsters propped back on their springs, the fog machines refilled. I had just about caught up when a third nightgown girl drifted directly into my path, held up a warning hand like a school crossing guard, and stopped me.

"No, no," I said. "I'm with her. I came with her." I stepped to the side, and the nightgown girl stepped with me. Her bare feet made cracking sounds in the snow-caked grass and left half-formed impressions. Her hand remained extended, blocking me. For several seconds, we stared at each other.

"They've been doing that since I got here," said Tricia, walking up next to me. "No one gets to go inside with the person they came with."

"Forget that," I said, ignoring Tricia, watching Kate. The nightgown guides on either side of her still held loosely to her arms, but they'd stopped walking, allowed her to turn around.

Kate's eyes were hooded in shadow. I couldn't tell if she was steeling herself or enjoying the whole thing or resigned or what. All she said was, "It's okay. It'll be fun."

"I came here with you," I said. "I want to go through it with you."

"Guess there are still at least a few things we don't get to go through together," said Kate. Then she smiled another of those wide, blooming smiles, but she aimed it at Tricia. "Take care of the poor professor. See you out the other side, David."

She stepped forward, surprising even the guides, I think. The one on the left lost her hold on Kate's arm. The house had a white front door with a giant ear-shaped brass handle that flashed in the icy moonlight. Kate closed her hand over it and glanced back one more time. She was still smiling. Then the door was open, and the blackness inside seemed to spill, for just a second, into the lawn. The door closed, and Kate was gone.

"It's not even fair," Tricia said. "I've been here longer than you guys."

"How long *have* you been here, anyway?" I muttered, unable

to pry my eyes from the door. The dark in there had seemed almost solid.

"Half an hour, maybe? There doesn't seem to be an order, though. They just come and get you. They got Robert maybe fifteen minutes ago."

"They make you go alone?"

"Some people. Some get to go in groups of two or three. Just not anyone you came here with. Think that's part of the plan? A way of making you uncomfortable or something?"

If it was, I thought, it was working. "Show me the game-booth," I said, mostly because I didn't like standing staring at the door. And somehow, I suspected I wouldn't be summoned as long as I did so.

I had my hands in my pockets, my arms tucked in tight at my sides because I thought Tricia might take my elbow or something, and I didn't want her to. But she just flicked her red-hatted head in the direction of the backyard, smiled at me, and walked off. I followed, watching the house, listening for screaming, but there was none. There was no sound at all. Other people, I thought, must have gone in before Kate and joined her to form a group, because there were only four or five hauntees left in the yard now.

A long, folding table lined the back of the first game booth, and on the table sat a row of foot-high stuffed elephants, all crouched back on their haunches with their trunks in the air. The elephants seemed disconcerting only in their ordinariness. Once again, I was confronted with the contradictions of this place, the completely unique and elaborately controlled atmosphere and the utterly prosaic imagery. Surely, finding and playing this particular game deserved more significant reward.

Leaning against the table, smoking a cigarette, stood a gray-haired, stooped old man in a cloak. He had his chin tilted back, his eyes aimed at the roof of the booth. For a second, I thought he might be impersonating the stuffed elephants, and I started to smile. The old man lowered rheumy, red-streaked gray eyes and looked at me, then Tricia. "Only one play per traveler," he said, his voice more smoke than sound.

"I'm not playing," said Tricia, cheerful as ever. "He is."

"Oh," said the old man, and dropped his cigarette to his feet where it hissed in the grass. "Spin the wheel," he said to me. "Test your fate."

The wheel sat on another folding table that ran along the front of the booth, looking as though it had been ripped from a Life game board and enlarged. It was made of white plastic roughly three feet in diameter. Positioned underneath the indicator was a circular piece of black construction paper. There was a single wedge of red paper taped over the black, at roughly high noon, with white lettering on it. The lettering read: SPINNER WINS ELEPHANT. There was lettering on the much larger black section of the circle, too. It said: DEALER LOSES HAND.

"I won Robert an elephant," Tricia told me.

I put my fingers on the wheel, then jerked them back. The spinner wasn't plastic; it was bone. And freezing.

"Jesus Christ," I said.

"Oops," said Tricia, laughing happily to herself. "Forgot to mention that, didn't I?"

The gray man was no longer looking at us. He was looking beyond us. Remembering his training, I supposed. I put my hand back on the spinner, glanced at Tricia, thought of Kate, and spun the wheel.

Around and around it whirred. It made no sound. The indicator circled the grid, and eventually glided to a stop deep in the black.

"No elephant for me," I said.

Sighing, the old man dropped his arm on the table in front of me. With his other hand, he withdrew a hacksaw from inside his coat, sighed again, shrugged. Then he drove the hacksaw straight down into his wrist, straight through to the table, where it vibrated a few seconds in the frozen wood.

"Holy *fuck!*" said Tricia, and flew backwards.

I stared at the hand on the table, severed now, a single, long tendon dangling from it like a tongue. The old man was staring at the hand, too. Mouth working, I took a step back. It had happened so fast that I couldn't quite grasp it yet. But there was no blood. No blood. Exquisitely realistic tendon, but no blood.

"You're awfully good," I said to the man.

He nodded, lifted a garbage bag from under the table, and swept the severed hand into it with his stump. Then he retreated to the back of the booth, placed a fresh cigarette between his lips, wiggled the stump into a pocket in his cloak, and reassumed his position.

"Oh, my God," Tricia said, and now she did grab my arm and held onto it as she went on laughing. Her laughter was irresistible, infectious, like a tickle. I felt myself burst into a smile.

We stayed arm in arm, watching the carnival booth, waiting to see what happened when the next *traveler*, as the man had called us, came to play. I at least wanted to see if the gray man had new fake hands in his cloak and could attach them without turning away and blocking our vision. But a scant minute later, the nightgown ghosts appeared, one on either side of us.

"Finally," Tricia breathed.

"You're sure you're up for this?" I asked, feeling almost giddy now. I couldn't wait to tell Kate about the booth. I couldn't wait to find her again. Besides, teasing Tricia was as irresistible as laughing with her.

Of course, she was better at teasing. "I've got my big, bad

prof," she said, squeezing my arm. I blushed, and she looked at me, and we let the nightgown ghosts lead us back around the long red house toward the white door, the waiting dark.

I had two wild, ridiculous thoughts as I was lead up the stoop. The first was that I'd just met Judge Albert Aloysius Dark, that he'd found the fountain of youth somewhere and decided to spend his eternity huddled away on the plains, plotting yearly appearances with selected friends. The faintly perverse, perpetually bored Santa Claus of Halloween. The second thought I said aloud.

"Where's the exit?" I said.

"What?" said Tricia.

"You said Robert went in, what, twenty minutes ago now? Where did he come out?"

"I thought of that."

"Did you think of an answer?"

Tricia grinned. "After you, Professor R."

One last time, I considered the possibility that this was all a hoax, the best ever perpetrated, at least on me. God, even Brian Tidrow could be a hoax, I thought, then dismissed the thought. I glanced at Tricia's face. Her red mouth hung open just a little, and her blue eyes were bright. This was no joke. None she was in on, anyway.

I took the handle, which, to my relief, felt like a door handle, and shoved. The door didn't creak but swung smoothly back. I glanced over my shoulder and gasped and stumbled forward, dragging Tricia behind me. The nightgown ghosts had been right on top of us, brushing against our backs. One of them smiled blankly at me, put her hand on the handle, and pulled the door closed.

For a minute, maybe more, we just stood in the dark. I kept waiting for my eyes to adjust, but there was nothing to adjust to.

This was blackness and silence, plain and simple. My ears almost stretched off my head, searching out sounds of people scrambling into place, spring triggers being set. Then they searched for just plain breathing, the tap of snow against outside shingles, anything at all. But there was nothing. Stepping into that foyer was like stepping into a coffin. Worse, actually. It was like walking completely out of the world.

"Professor R.?" I heard Tricia whisper. Somehow, I'd lost her elbow, but I felt her hand crawl up my sleeve now, take hold of me.

"Right here," I said, though I was at least as happy to hear and feel her as she must have been me. I found myself hoping, desperately, that Kate had been allowed some sort of group to go through this with. The idea of her standing here this long, with Brian Tidrow's blown-apart head leering under her eyelids, was more than I could bear.

The house's first overture was a touch. It was so subtle that I mistook it, for a moment, for Tricia's breath near my cheek. But then I realized I could feel it on my hands, too, a gentle, intermittent rushing of air. The first warm anything I'd encountered since the car heater.

It did feel like breath, though. As if there were dozens of people crouched right up against us, just breathing.

"Hey," I said, because even as I'd had that thought, I knew it wasn't true. Because I realized I could see, a little. Something, somewhere, was casting a faint green glow. I glanced toward Tricia, saw her outline.

Tricia glanced back at me. "I can see you," she said.

"Feel better?" I said.

"Nope." Even in that dim light, I could see her teeth.

"Smart girl."

We were in a sort of hangar, long and wide and empty. There

was a doorway, however, fifteen feet away on the left. The glow came from there. The little puffs of air came from everywhere, but the glow was on the left.

I tugged Tricia's arm, and we started that way. Nothing dropped out of the ceiling. Nothing moved at all. As we approached the opening, I noted the crawling pace we adopted. Walking a haunted house properly is a lot like making love, I'd decided years ago. Maximum enjoyment requires concentration, the patience to allow for moments of electric, teasing agony, a suspension of disbelief in your own boundaries, and most of all, a willingness to pay attention. Despite my yearly visits to every spook joint in Clarkston, I hadn't paid so much attention since high school. Despite and because of everything, I smiled. We stepped into a hallway that ran ahead for fifty feet or so and then jogged to the right.

"See, they understand, these people," I said. "You don't need fog. You don't need rubber hatchets in your head and things lunging out and grabbing your hair. You just need the dark and the silence and some imagination and—"

"No lectures, Professor," said Tricia.

My smile widened unconsciously. "But lecturing makes me feel better."

"Exactly," said Tricia, and I could see her eyes flashing. Her concentration on this moment was total. She led me forward, and I let her.

We'd gone perhaps fifteen feet when my foot hit the floor and sank, and I jerked it back. I hadn't sunk far, but I didn't like the squishiness where wood or cement should have been. I'd seen and felt and imagined too many bones tonight. I thought of the soft spot on a baby's skull and shuddered. I lifted my foot again, put it down to the left of where I'd put it before. It sank again.

"Is this carpet?" Tricia asked.

"No idea."

"Feels gross."

"And you didn't even know Brian Tidrow."

"What?"

"Just walk, Tricia. Let's walk."

It was like I'd imagined stepping onto the moors would be, as a child, after I'd been read my first story with quicksand in it. For weeks I'd been terrified of walking in the grass. I'd had such total, unwavering faith until then in the ground.

Sometimes our feet hit solid surface. Sometimes the surface gave, depressing downward a little. This might not even be an intended effect, I decided. This could just be old, rotting wood. I didn't believe it, though.

As soon as we reached the spot where the passageway veered, the glow became a full-fledged spill of light from another doorway ten yards ahead. Without a word, we turned that way and crept forward. The floor beneath us became solid again. The rushes of air diminished, then disappeared altogether. But there were other sounds, now. Rustlings from down the hall, and a sort of drip and slosh from nowhere in particular. If the night had been warmer, I'd have assumed that ice was melting off the roof outside.

No sound came from the room with the doorway, though. We reached it side by side, turned toward it together, and Tricia said, "Oh" and started to giggle and stopped. The effect was delayed on me, too, because the whole thing had been so studiously constructed to look real, rather than ghoulish.

On the ceiling in the center of the room, right where a light fixture should have been, a shining metal hook glinted in the seemingly sourceless green light. From the hook, not swinging, hung a slightly pudgy, pale boy, maybe eight years old. The noose around his neck, right above the collar of his Minnesota Twins baseball jersey, appeared to have bitten straight through his skin into his muscles and veins, which you could just see, little red tangles in yellow twists of twine. His tongue didn't bulge and it wasn't blue. It just drooped out the side of his lips in a peculiarly childlike way, like the untucked tail of a shirt. The boy's bare feet were at least half a yard off the floor.

A red velvet rope barred Tricia and me from entering the room. But we stood a while, waiting for the kid to blink, yell "Boo," jerk forward, do any of those comforting haunted-house things. But he didn't. He just hung.

Back down the hall, I heard the thud of boot on floor. I looked that way, saw a person-shaped bulk detach itself from the massing shadows and step toward us.

"Time to go, I think," I said.

"Professor R.?" Tricia said. For the first time in my experience of her, she sounded like a teenage girl.

"Let's just keep walking." I'm not sure which of us took the other's hand. "Just imagine the stories we're going to be telling on Monday."

"Monday?" said Tricia. "Shit, I'm calling everyone I've ever met as soon as I get home."

Twenty steps ahead, the passageway ended in a T. To the right, we could see one more strip of light, flickering and yellow, down near the floor this time, so we went that way. Soon we realized we were approaching a plain wooden door, pulled most of the way shut. My least-favorite door position. At least when a door is completely closed, you assume that nothing will come out to you. I heard footfall again, glanced back, saw the person-shaped shadow reach the T in the hallway and turn in our direction. Whoever he was moved just slightly more slowly than we did. But he kept coming.

We were a few feet from the door when the grunting began. For a single second, simply because we'd heard virtually nothing since we entered, it startled me. Then I started to smile. The grunt was distinctly human. Human-playing-ape.

"Oooh," it went. "Oooh-oooh."

I started to say something to Tricia and finally noticed the pajama child cloaked in the black shadows near the door. As soon as I saw him, he took a step forward. He was a bit older than the hanging boy, with long hair that lay in a black, wriggling mass on his shoulders and made his head appear encased in snakes. It could have been a wig. His pajamas were yellow and baggy.

"Watch the gorilla," he said flatly, pushed the door open just a bit more, and stepped back into the shadows, his movements precise and mechanical, like the robot pirates at Disneyland.

"Gorillas scare me," said Tricia.

"Now, have you ever taken the time to sit down and talk to one?" I said, and she elbowed me in the ribs. The pressure of my coat against me reminded me that I wasn't warm. Apparently, the house had not been heated.

Right as we reached the door, I saw the cage on the other side of it, and for the third time experienced a flicker of disappointment. The cage had been dug into the wall, lit by torches that guttered in sconces. In the cage, "ooh-oohing," was a tallish person in an old and painfully obvious gorilla suit.

"Okay," I said, and started forward, pushing the door all the way back. The gorilla guy lunged at his bars, jammed one rubber arm through at us, grunted. My pride was up. I stared right into his eyes, tugged Tricia beside me, strolled past. When the second gorilla dropped on us from behind, I flew fifteen feet down the hall and shouted. Tricia screamed. Then both of us whirled, stunned, laughing.

The second gorilla stood in the passageway, hunched, huge, panting. He did not say "ooh." His skin still didn't look quite real, but it didn't look rubber, either. Mostly, it looked unhealthy, clinging in strips to whoever was underneath there like black, desiccated mummy wrapping.

"Classic misdirection," I panted. "That guy was just sitting there on the wall if we'd looked, see? But they got us focused on the one in the cage."

"You're doing it again, Professor."

"That's because that scared me shitless, Tricia."

"I noticed that."

The door behind the gorillas creaked. Something else was pushing through. The shadow that had been herding us along, I suspected.

"On we go," said Tricia, pulling me forward, and we continued down the hall.

We walked twenty paces, then twenty more. I began to wonder just how big this house was. It hadn't looked forty paces long in any direction from the outside. Nevertheless, we'd gone nearly a hundred before we hit the stairwell.

The architects of this funhouse had thoughtfully provided a single torch, licking the wall at eye level, to alert passersby that they could plunge to their deaths here. Maybe this house had been built on the prairie because it was outside the jurisdiction of Clarkston's increasingly specific and stringent haunted-house safety code.

"We in the right place?" Tricia said.

I thought about that. "The only way to know for sure is to wait and make sure the big thing behind us catches up."

"Or we could keep going."

The stairs were cement, but ten steps down, the walls lost their comforting wooden skin, became dirt. Ahead was a floor, or at least a landing, and the stairwell banked to the left into total darkness.

I stopped, listened, hissed for Tricia to stop too. For the second time, and much more loudly now, I heard the dripping, sloshing sound. It came from ahead of us.

"Maybe we *are* going the wrong way," I said.

"I don't think so," Tricia murmured, her eyes raised above my head, and I turned and saw the shadow-shape fill the doorway. Whatever it was wore a black cowl, complete with hood, and it was big. Six and a half feet tall, at least. I couldn't see its face. But it was carrying a gavel.

"Okay," I said. "Down, Tricia."

Down we went. The shape stayed where it was until we reached the landing, then took a single step after us. Tricia reached the landing first.

"What's below us?" I called, catching up.

"More stairs," said Tricia, and the torch behind us went out. "Fuck."

"Let's go. Forward is homeward."

"Arm, please, Professor R."

I gave her my arm. We continued down. Five steps. Ten. Down, down, down. Every few seconds, we heard a single creak as the Judge-thing in the cowl pursued at its leisurely pace.

From deep inside me, a laugh swelled. I felt it crest in the back of my throat, then break into the open air.

"Oh my God, shut up," said Tricia.

But I kept on laughing. Truly, I thought, this was the best I'd ever seen. Then my foot plunged ankle deep into water, and I shouted and teetered backward.

"*Gross!*" Tricia yelled. She fell back beside me, shaking her leg, and we lay together on the steps.

Somewhere above us, a stair creaked.

"Kate hates puddles," I said, trying to imagine her coming through this. Abruptly, I had no laughter left. I was just overwhelmingly tired. And Brian Tidrow was dead. I hadn't liked him. I liked his being dead even less.

"What if they just lead everyone down here and drown them?" Tricia murmured.

"That would lower my overall rating of the experience," I said, trying to rouse myself to push ahead. How much longer, really, could all this be?

"We could be walking in a sewer."

"There aren't many people out here, though. So the amount of actual sewage—"

"Shut up, Professor R.," said Tricia. But she laughed, or at least expelled the air she'd been clutching in her teeth.

I got up. Tricia got up, too, and the stairs above us creaked again. But there was no light to see by. Gritting my teeth, I stepped straight down into the wet, tugging Tricia behind me. The floor underneath was solid, anyway. Tricia moaned as her ankles sank, but she didn't say anything. We went forward.

Mostly, for the first few feet, I was listening. I wanted to hear where the water we disturbed rolled into a wall, thinking maybe I could judge the size of this tunnel, space, whatever it was. But I couldn't.

"Tell me this is water," Tricia whispered.

"Hadn't even thought of that. Thanks, Tricia." I shuddered. I was whispering, too.

We'd gone another fifteen steps when overhead lights burst to life, blinding us, and shut off just as quickly, igniting fireworks on my retina. I stopped hard, the water sloshed, and the disturbed dark flapped and fluttered around us.

"Now what?" Tricia said.

"Let's see if that happens again. Maybe we can see where we are."

We waited maybe a minute, which felt like twenty. Nothing happened. Shrugging, I tugged Tricia's arm, took a step, and the lights bloomed, held a split second longer this time, and died.

"Hmmm," I said, and started forward again.

Five steps later, the water got deeper. It happened in a quick, slipping slope, and we were up to our knees, then nearly our waists. I continued to insist to myself that it was water. At least it wasn't cold. If anything, it was a little too warm.

This time when the lights flashed, they stayed on a good five seconds. My pupils telescoped, my brain locked, and I got just a glimpse of wooden walls to the sides, and another staircase less than fifty feet ahead, leading up. Then the dark slammed down.

"Okay. Exit ho," I said, and felt the first bump against my leg. "Uh-oh."

"What?" said Tricia.

"Just walk."

"Hey," Tricia said, and then, *"Jesus.* There's something—"

"Walk, Tricia. Wait for the lights."

"I don't want to see."

The lights exploded. I was watching the water. I very nearly fainted into it.

Drifting on the black, rippling surface were fingers. Thumbs. Dozens of them. Hundreds, floating like dead fish in a dynamited pond. I saw part of an ear. The lights went out.

"Professor," Tricia said, her voice very small. "Did you see—"

"Walk, Tricia. Fast."

Mercifully, the water got shallower just a few steps farther on, but the things in the water swirled more thickly around us. I kept my hands locked against my chest and burrowed straight ahead. Tricia was even faster, very nearly running as we scrambled up another slope. The water level fell toward our knees.

Both of us heard slower, steadier sloshing behind us. But when the lights came on again, neither of us glanced back.

Seconds later, we were on the stairs, breathing hard. I might have bent over and kissed the firm, dry wood beneath me except that my pants were soaked and felt awful when my skin pressed against them. Walking sopping wet across the frozen prairie to the car would be fun, I thought.

But worth it. The whole damn thing had been more than worth it. I couldn't wait to grab Kate, hold her, laugh with her. I couldn't wait to start digging around town for wood-purchasing and electricity records in the hopes of tracking down the creators of all this. I couldn't wait to interview Robert Hayright and everyone else who'd been here about exactly what they'd seen. For the first time in years, I felt like writing.

More than anything else, though, I felt grateful. All my life, I'd considered myself a sort of library phantom, haunting the graveyards and record morgues of my own history without ever, somehow, materializing inside it. But I was soaking in it, now, shivering in the relentless, terrifying rush of it.

I looked up and saw the exit sign glowing plainly, redly, twenty steps above me.

"That's it?" Tricia clutched her arms against herself and held her sopping pant-legs very still.

"Are you joking?" I answered, but I knew what she meant. I didn't want to leave. I wanted to go on being this kind of scared forever.

Except that I didn't really want the Judge-thing to catch us. So when I heard him sloshing closer, I started up the steps. I had reached the landing, halfway to the top, when the strobe light strafed us, and the pajama people stepped out of the wall on either side of the staircase. There were two on every stair.

"Bummer," I said, because I knew this trick. I'd seen it in half the haunted houses I'd ever visited. True, I was impressed by the doors cleverly carved into the walls to hide all these people until we were right on top of them. But now, I was going to start up the stairs, and the pajama-people would produce hatchets and clubs and raise them, slowly, looking all lurchy in the twitches of light, and then they'd lean in and menace us as we made for the door.

"Ohhh!" I heard Tricia moan. I also heard a slosh and then drip from below, and I knew that the Judge-thing had reached the foot of the stairs.

"No worries," I muttered, and, ignoring the wetness in my legs, started upward again.

"I hate strobes," said Tricia. But I heard her stepping behind me.

I had my hands in my pockets. As I passed the pajama-people, I glared straight into their eyes. The only thing that surprised me was that none of them made any sort of mock-threatening motion. In fact, they didn't move at all. They just stood, silent as heralds in a painting of a medieval procession, and watched me go.

"Unnh," I heard Tricia say, and looked back, and everything went to hell.

Full-blown, blazing, ordinary light flooded the space down there, more than enough for me to see the Judge-thing. He had not actually stepped onto the staircase, and was instead standing knee-deep in the black pool of wetness we'd traversed. I couldn't see his face because of his cowl. But I could see the fingers and thumbs floating around him.

They were moving.

Dozens of them clung to the fringe of his cloak or crawled blindly up his hanging arms, wriggling. Like bees over a bee-keeper, I thought wildly, and my breath flew from me, and

Tricia screamed and shoved me out of the way and hurtled out the exit door.

Staggering, I tore my eyes from the Judge-thing and stumbled up the last few stairs. Still, the pajama people made no move to hold me. Tricia had left the door half open in her flight, and I scrambled for it, very nearly tumbling to my knees. Three steps more. Two.

Then I was out, in a sort of clearing on the prairie, several hundred feet from the red house, and the door was starting to shut, and a crushing burst of desperate longing exploded through me. For a split second, I thought it was for the house. The knowledge that I would never experience another like it. That the eternal Halloween search of the lifelong Clarkstonian was over for me.

Then I realized what had been so strange about Tricia's flight from the house. Or rather, the moment just before it. When she'd screamed, she hadn't been looking at the Judge-thing. She was looking into the shadows right beside her. And the look on her face wasn't terror, or not only terror. It was also recognition.

I knew, then. I knew even before I turned around. And I thought I understood at least a little. The wriggling fingers. The Judge-thing, and the nature of its power. The barefoot pajama boys, and the decrepit gorilla. Not why. Not how. But something. And I knew the plains weren't empty after all, not the way we'd thought all these years. In fact, they are overflowing, overrun with Native Americans, homesteaders, dancing girls, ranchers, Chinese, buffalo. All the murdered, restless dead.

I watched Kate watch me from the top of the stairs. She hadn't been issued her pajamas yet, I guessed. Her coat was open, at last, and there was no blanket around her, and I could finally see the hole Brian Tidrow must have blown in her stomach, just as she walked in his door, in the seconds before he'd shot his own head off.

"No," I said.

"Good-bye, David," Kate said softly, and the door swung closed as she blew me a kiss.

Dancing Men

*"These are the
last days of our lives
so we give a signal
maybe there still
will be relatives
or acquaintances
of these persons...
They were tortured
and burnt goodbye..."*

—Testimonial found at Chelmno

W e'd been all afternoon in the Old Jewish Cemetery, where green light filters through the trees and lies atop the tumbled tombstones like algae. Mostly I think the kids were tired. The two-week Legacy of the Holocaust tour I had organized had taken us to Zeppelin Field in Nuremberg, where downed electrical wires slither through the brittle grass, and Bebelplatz in East Berlin, where ghost-shadows of burned books flutter in their chamber in the ground like white wings. We'd spent our nights not sleeping on sleeper trains east to Auschwitz and Birkenau and our days on public transport, traipsing through the fields of dead and the monuments to them, and all seven high-school juniors in my care had had enough.

From my spot on a bench alongside the roped-off stone path that meandered through the grounds and back out to the streets of Josefov, I watched six of my seven charges giggling and chattering around the final resting place of Rabbi Loew. I'd told them the story of the rabbi, and the clay man he'd supposedly created and then animated, and now they were running their hands over his tombstone, tracing Hebrew letters they couldn't read, chanting *"Emet,"* the word I'd taught them, in low voices and laughing. As of yet, nothing had risen from the dirt. The Tribe, they'd taken to calling themselves, after I told them that the Wandering Jews didn't really work, historically, since the essential characteristic of the Wanderer himself was his solitude.

There are teachers, I suppose, who would have been considered members of the Tribe by the Tribe, particularly on a summer trip, far from home and school and television and familiar language. But I had never been that sort of teacher.

Nor was I the only excluded member of our traveling party. Lurking not far from me, I spotted Penny Berry, the quietest member of our group and the only Goy, staring over the graves into the trees with her expressionless eyes half closed and her lipstickless lips curled into the barest hint of a smile. Her auburn hair sat cocked on the back of her head in a tight, precise ponytail. When she saw me watching, she wandered over, and I swallowed a sigh. It wasn't that I didn't like Penny, exactly. But she asked uncomfortable questions, and she knew how to wait for answers, and she made me nervous for no reason I could explain.

"Hey, Mr. Gadeuszki," she said, her enunciation studied, perfect. She'd made me teach her how to say it right, grind the s and z and k together into that single, Slavic snarl of sound. "What's with the stones?"

She gestured at the tiny gray pebbles placed across the tops of several nearby tombstones. Those on the slab nearest us glinted in the warm, green light like little eyes. "In memory," I said. I thought about sliding over on the bench to make room for her, then thought that would only make both of us even more awkward.

"Why not flowers?" Penny said.

I sat still, listening to the clamor of new-millennium Prague just beyond the stone wall that enclosed the cemetery. "Jews bring stones."

A few minutes later, when she realized I wasn't going to say anything else, Penny moved off in the general direction of the Tribe. I watched her go and allowed myself a few more peaceful seconds. Probably, I thought, it was time to move us along. We had the astronomical clock left to see today, puppet-theater tickets for tonight, the plane home to Cleveland in the morning. And just because the kids were tired didn't mean they would tolerate loitering here much longer. For seven summers in a row, I had taken students on some sort of exploring trip. "Because you've got nothing better to do," one member of the Tribe cheerfully informed me one night the preceding week. Then he'd said, "Oh my God, I was just kidding, Mr. G."

And I'd had to reassure him that I knew he was, I always looked like that.

"That's true. You do," he'd said, and returned to his tripmates.

Now, I rubbed my hand over the stubble on my shaven scalp, stood, and blinked as my family name—in its original Polish spelling—flashed behind my eyelids again, looking just the way it had this morning amongst all the other names etched into the Pinkas Synagogue wall. The ground went slippery underneath me, the tombstones slid sideways in the grass, and I teetered and sat down hard.

When I lifted my head and opened my eyes, the Tribe had swarmed around me, a whirl of backwards baseball caps and tanned legs and Nike symbols. "I'm fine," I said quickly, stood up, and to my relief I found I did feel fine. I had no idea what had just happened. "Slipped."

"Kind of," said Penny Berry from the edges of the group, and I avoided looking her way.

"Time to go, gang. Lots more to see."

It has always surprised me when they do what I say, because mostly, they do. It's not me, really. The social contract between teachers and students may be the oldest mutually accepted enacted ritual on this earth, and its power is stronger than most people imagine.

We passed between the last of the graves and through a low stone opening. The dizziness or whatever it had been was gone, and I felt only a faint tingling in my fingertips as I drew my last breath of that too-heavy air, thick with loam and grass springing from bodies stacked a dozen deep in the ground.

The side street beside the Old-New Synagogue was crammed with tourists, their purses and backpacks open like the mouths of grotesquely overgrown chicks. Into those open mouths went wooden puppets and embroidered kipot and Chamsa hands from the rows of stalls that lined the sidewalk; the walls, I thought, of an all new, much more ingenious sort of ghetto. In a way, this place had become exactly what Hitler had meant for it to be: the Museum of a Dead Race, only the paying customers were descendants of the Race, and they spent money in amounts he could never have dreamed. The ground had begun to roll under me again, and I closed my eyes. When I opened them, the tourists had cleared in front of me, and I saw the stall, a lopsided wooden hulk on bulky brass wheels. It tilted toward me, the puppets nailed to its side leering and chattering while the gypsy leaned out from between them, nose studded with a silver star, grinning.

He touched the toy nearest him, set it rocking on its terrible, thin wire. *"Loh-oot-kovay deevahd-low,"* he said, and then I was down, flat on my face in the street.

I don't know how I wound up on my back. Somehow, somebody had rolled me over. I couldn't breathe. My stomach felt squashed, as though there was something squatting on it, wooden and heavy, and I jerked, gagged, opened my eyes, and the light blinded me.

"I didn't," I said, blinking, brain flailing. I wasn't even sure I'd been all the way unconscious, couldn't have been out more than a few seconds. But the way the light affected my eyes, it was as though I'd been buried for a month.

"Doh-bree den, doh-bree den," said a voice over me, and I squinted, teared up, blinked into the gypsy's face, the one from the stall, and almost screamed. Then he touched my forehead, and he was just a man, red Manchester United cap on his head, black eyes kind as they hovered around mine. The cool hand he laid against my brow had a wedding ring on it, and the silver star in his nose caught the afternoon light.

I meant to say I was okay, but what came out was "I didn't" again. The gypsy said something else to me. The language could have been Czech or Slovakian or Romani. I didn't know enough to tell the difference, and my ears weren't working right. In them I could feel a painful, persistent pressure. The gypsy stood, and I saw my students clustered behind him like a knot I'd drawn taut. When they saw me looking, they burst out babbling, and I shook my head, tried to calm them, and then I felt their hands on mine, pulling me to a sitting position. The world didn't spin. The ground stayed still. The puppet stall I would not look at kept its distance.

"Mr. G., are you all right?" one of them asked, her voice shrill, slipping toward panic.

Then Penny Berry knelt beside me and looked straight into me, and I could see her formidable brain churning behind those placid eyes, the silvery color of Lake Erie when it's frozen.

"Didn't what?" she asked.

And I answered, because I had no choice. "Kill my grandfather."

2

They propped me at my desk in our pension not far from the Charles Bridge and brought me a glass of "nice water," which was one of our traveling jokes. It was what the too-thin waitress at Terezin—the "town presented to the Jews by the Nazis," as the old propaganda film we saw at the museum proclaimed—thought we were saying when we asked for ice.

For a while, the Tribe sat on my bed and talked quietly to each other and refilled my glass for me. But after thirty minutes or so, when I hadn't keeled over again and wasn't babbling and seemed my usual sullen, solid, bald self, they started shuffling around, playing with my curtains, ignoring me. One of them threw a pencil at another. For a short while, I almost forgot about the nausea churning in my stomach, the trembling in my wrists, the puppets bobbing on their wires in my head.

"Hey," I said. I had to say it twice more to get their attention. I usually do.

Finally, Penny noticed and said, "Mr. Gadeuszki's trying to say something," and they slowly quieted down.

I put my quivering hands on my lap under the desk and left them there. "Why don't you kids get back on the metro and go see the astronomical clock?"

The Tribe members looked at each other uncertainly. "Really," I told them. "I'm fine. When's the next time you're going to be in Prague?"

They were good kids, and they looked unsure for a few seconds longer. In the end, though, they started trickling toward the door, and I thought I'd gotten them out until Penny Berry stepped in front of me.

"You killed your grandfather," she said.

"Didn't," I snarled, and Penny blinked, and everyone whirled to stare at me. I took a breath, almost got control of my voice. "I said I didn't kill him."

"Oh," Penny said. She was on this trip not because of any familial or cultural heritage but because this was the most interesting experience she could find to devour this month. She was pressing me now because she suspected I had something more startling to share than Prague did at the moment. And she was always hungry.

Or maybe she was just lonely, confused about the kid she had never quite been and the world she didn't quite feel part of. Which would make her more than a little like me, and might explain why she had always annoyed me as much as she did.

"It's stupid," I said. "It's nothing."

Penny didn't move. In my memory, the little wooden man on his black pine branch quivered, twitched, and began to rock, side to side.

"I need to write it down," I said, trying to sound gentle. Then I lied. "Maybe I'll show you when I'm done."

Five minutes later, I was alone in my room with a fresh glass of nice water and there was sand on my tongue and desert sun on my neck and that horrid, gasping breathing like a snake rattle in my ears, and for the first time in many, many years, I was home.

3

In June 1978, on the day after school let out, I was sitting in my bedroom in Albuquerque, New Mexico, thinking about absolutely nothing when my dad came in and sat down on my bed and said, "I want you to do something for me."

In my nine years of life, my father had almost never asked me to do anything for him. As far as I could tell, he had very few things that he wanted. He worked at an insurance firm and came home at exactly 5:30 every night and played an hour of catch with me before dinner or, sometimes, walked me to the ice-cream shop. After dinner, he sat on the black couch in the den reading paperback mystery novels until 9:30. The paperbacks were all old, with bright yellow or red covers featuring men in trench coats and women with black dresses sliding down the curves in their bodies like tar. It made me nervous, sometimes, just watching my father's hands on the covers. I asked him once why he liked those kinds of books, and he shook his head. "All those people," he said, sounding, as usual, as though he was speaking to me through a tin can from a great distance. "Doing all those things." At exactly 9:30, every single night I can remember, my father clicked off the lamp next to the couch and touched me on the head if I was up and went to bed.

"What do you want me to do?" I asked that June morning, though I didn't much care. This was the first weekend of summer vacation, and I had months of free time in front of me, and I never knew quite what to do with it anyway.

"What I tell you, okay?" my father said.

Without even thinking, I said, "Sure."

And he said, "Good. I'll tell Grandpa you're coming." Then he left me gaping on the bed while he went into the kitchen to use the phone.

My grandfather lived seventeen miles from Albuquerque in a red adobe hut in the middle of the desert. The only sign of humanity anywhere around him was the ruins of a small pueblo maybe half a mile away. Even now, what I remember most about my grandfather's house is the desert rolling up to and through it in an endless red tide that never receded. From the back steps, I could see the pueblo honeycombed with caves like a giant bee-hive tipped on its side, empty of bees but buzzing as the wind whipped through it.

Four years before, my grandfather had told my parents to knock off the token visits. Then he'd had his phone shut off. As far as I knew, none of us had seen him since.

All my life, he'd been dying. He had emphysema and some kind of weird allergic condition that turned swatches of his skin pink. The last time I'd been with him, he'd just sat in a chair in a tank top breathing through a tube. He'd looked like a piece of petrified wood.

The next morning, a Sunday, my father packed my green

camp duffel bag with a box of new, unopened wax packs of baseball cards and the transistor radio my mother had given me for my birthday the year before, then loaded it and me into the grimy green Datsun he always meant to wash and never did. "Time to go," he told me in his mechanical voice, and I was still too baffled by what was happening to protest as he led me outside. Moments before, a morning thunderstorm had rocked the whole house, but now the sun was up, searing the whole sky orange. Our street smelled like creosote and green chili and adobe mud.

"I don't want to go," I said to my father.

"I wouldn't either, if I were you," he told me, and started the car.

"You don't even like him," I said.

My father just looked at me, and for an astonishing second, I thought he was going to hug me. But he looked away instead, dropped the car into gear, and drove us out of town.

All the way to my grandfather's house, we followed the thunderstorm. It must have been traveling at exactly our speed, because we never got any closer, and it never got farther away. It just retreated before us, a big black wall of nothing, like a shadow the whole world cast, and every now and then streaks of lightning flew up the clouds like signal flares and illuminated the sand and mountains and rain.

"Why are we doing this?" I asked when my dad started slowing, studying the sand on his side of the car for the dirt track that led to my grandfather's.

"Want to drive?" He gestured to me to slide across the seat into his lap.

Again, I was surprised. My dad always seemed willing enough to play catch with me. But he rarely generated ideas on his own for things we could do together. And the thought of sitting in his lap with his arms around me was too alien to fathom. I waited too long, and the moment passed. My father didn't ask again. Through the windshield, I looked at the wet road already drying in patches in the sun. The whole day felt distant, like someone else's dream.

"You know he was in the war, right?" my father said, and despite our crawling speed he had to jam on the brakes to avoid passing the turnoff. No one, it seemed to me, could possibly have intended this to be a road. It wasn't dug or flattened or marked, just a rumple in the earth.

"Yeah," I said.

That he'd been in the war was pretty much the only thing I knew about my grandfather. Actually, he'd been in the camps. After the war, he'd been in other camps in Israel for almost five years while Red Cross workers searched for living relatives and found none, and finally turned him loose to make his way as best he could.

As soon as we were off the highway, sand ghosts rose around the car, ticking against the trunk and hood as we passed. Thanks to the thunderstorm, they left a wet, red residue like bug smear on the hood and windshield.

"You know, now that I think about it," my father said, his voice flat as ever but the words clearer, somehow, and I found myself leaning closer to him to make sure I heard him over the churning wheels. "He was even less of a grandfather to you than a father to me." He rubbed a hand over the bald spot just beginning to spread over the top of his head like an egg yolk being squashed. I'd never seen him do that before. It made him look old.

My grandfather's house rose out of the desert like a druid mound. There was no shape to it. It had exactly one window, and that couldn't be seen from the road. No mailbox. Never in my life, I realized abruptly, had I had to sleep in there.

"Dad, please don't make me stay," I said as he stopped the car fifteen feet or so from the front door.

He looked at me, and his mouth turned down a little, and his shoulders tensed. Then he sighed. "Three days," he said, and got out.

"*You* stay," I said, but I got out, too.

When I was standing beside him, looking past the house at the distant pueblo, he said, "Your grandfather didn't ask for me, he asked for you. He won't hurt you. And he doesn't ask for much from us, or from anyone."

"Neither do you."

After a while, and very slowly, as though remembering how, my father smiled. "And neither do you, Seth."

Neither the smile nor the statement reassured me.

"Just remember this, son. Your grandfather has had a very hard life, and not just because of the camps. He worked two jobs for twenty-five years to provide for my mother and me. He never called in sick. He never took vacations. And he was ecstatic when you were born."

That surprised me. "Really? How do you know?"

For the first time I could remember, my father blushed, and I thought maybe I'd caught him lying, and then I wasn't sure. He kept looking at me. "Well, he came to town, for one thing. Twice."

For a little longer, we stood together while the wind rolled over the rocks and sand. I couldn't smell the rain anymore, but I thought I could taste it, a little. Tall, leaning cacti prowled the waste around us like stick figures who'd escaped from one of my doodles. I was always doodling, then, trying to get the shapes of things.

Finally, the thin, wooden door to the adobe clicked open, and out stepped Lucy, and my father straightened and put his hand on his bald spot again and put it back down.

She didn't live there, as far as I knew. But I'd never been to my grandfather's house when she wasn't in it. I knew she worked for some foundation that provided care to Holocaust victims, though she was Navajo, not Jewish, and that she'd been coming out here all my life to make my grandfather's meals, bathe him, keep him company. I rarely saw them speak to each other. When I was little and my grandmother was still alive and we were still welcome, Lucy used to take me to the pueblo after she'd finished with my grandfather and watch me climb around on the stones and peer into the empty caves and listen to the wind chase thousand-year-old echoes out of the walls.

There were gray streaks now in the black hair that poured down Lucy's shoulders, and I could see semicircular lines like tree rings in her dark, weathered cheeks. But I was uncomfortably aware, this time, of the way her breasts pushed her plain white denim shirt out of the top of her jeans while her eyes settled on mine, black and still.

"Thank you for coming," she said, as if I'd had a choice. When I didn't answer, she looked at my father. "Thank you for bringing him. We're set up out back."

I threw one last questioning glance at my father as Lucy started away, but he just looked bewildered or bored or whatever he generally was. And that made me angry. " 'Bye," I told him, and moved toward the house.

"Good-bye," I heard him say, and something in his tone unsettled me; it was too sad. I shivered, turned around, and my father said, "He want to see me?"

He looked thin, I thought, just another spindly cactus, holding my duffel bag out from his side. If he'd been speaking to me, I might have run to him. I wanted to. But he was watching Lucy, who had stopped at the edge of the square of patio cement outside the front door.

"I don't think so," she said, and came over to me and took my hand. Without another word, my father tossed my duffel bag onto the miniature patio and climbed back in his car. For a moment, his eyes caught mine through the windshield, and I said, "Wait," but my father didn't hear me. I said it louder, and Lucy put her hand on my shoulder.

"This has to be done, Seth," she said.

"What does?"

"This way." She gestured toward the other side of the house, and I followed her there and stopped when I saw the hogan.

It sat next to the squat gray cactus I'd always considered the edge of my grandfather's yard. It looked surprisingly solid, its mud walls dry and gray and hard, its pocked, stumpy wooden pillars firm in the ground, almost as if they were real trees that had somehow taken root there.

"You live here now?" I blurted, and Lucy stared at me.

"Oh, yes, Seth. Me sleep-um ground. *How.*" She pulled aside the hide curtain at the front of the hogan and ducked inside, and I followed.

I thought it would be cooler in there, but it wasn't. The wood and mud trapped the heat but blocked the light. I didn't like it. It reminded me of an oven, of Hansel and Gretel. And it reeked of the desert: burnt sand, hot wind, nothingness.

"This is where you'll sleep," Lucy said. "It's also where we'll work." She knelt and lit a beeswax candle and placed it in the center of the dirt floor in a scratched glass drugstore candlestick. "We need to begin right now."

"Begin what?" I asked, fighting down another shudder as the candlelight played over the room. Against the far wall, tucked under a miniature canopy constructed of metal poles and a tarpaulin, were a sleeping bag and a pillow. My bed, I assumed. Beside it sat a low, rolling table, and on the table were another candlestick, a cracked ceramic bowl, some matches, and the Dancing Man.

In my room in the pension in the Czech Republic, five thousand miles and twenty years removed from that place, I put my pen down and swallowed the entire glass of lukewarm water my students had left me. Then I got up and went to the window, staring out at the trees and the street. I was hoping to see my kids returning like ducks to a familiar pond, flapping their arms and jostling each other and squawking and laughing. Instead, I saw my own face, faint and featureless, too white in the window glass. I went back to the desk and picked up the pen.

The Dancing Man's eyes were all pupil, carved in two perfect ovals in the knottiest wood I had ever seen. The nose was just a notch, but the mouth was enormous, a giant O, like the opening of a cave. I was terrified of the thing even before I noticed that it was moving.

Moving, I suppose, is too grand a description. It . . . leaned. First one way, then the other, on a bent black pine branch that ran straight through its belly. In a fit of panic, after a nightmare, I described it to my college roommate, a physics major, and he shrugged and said something about perfect balance and pendulums and gravity and the rotation of the earth. For the first and only time, right in that first moment, I lifted the branch off the table, and the Dancing Man leaned a little faster, weaving to the beat of my blood. I put the branch down fast.

"Take the drum," Lucy said behind me, and I ripped my eyes away from the Dancing Man.

"What?" I said.

She gestured at the table, and I realized she meant the ceramic bowl. I didn't understand, and I didn't want to go over there. But I didn't know what else to do, and I felt ridiculous under Lucy's stare.

The Dancing Man was at the far end of its branch, leaning, mouth open. Trying to be casual, I snatched the bowl from underneath it and retreated to where Lucy knelt. The water inside the bowl made a sloshing sound but didn't splash out, and I held it away from my chest in surprise and noticed the covering stitched over the top. It was hide of some kind, moist when I touched it.

"Like this," said Lucy, and she leaned close and tapped on the skin of the drum. The sound was deep and tuneful, like a voice. I sat down next to Lucy. She tapped again, in a slow, repeating pattern. I put my hands where hers had been, and when she nodded at me, I began to play.

" 'Okay?' I said.

"Harder." Lucy reached into her pocket and pulled out a long wooden stick. The candlelight flickered across the stick, and I saw the carving. A pine tree, and underneath it, roots that bulged along the base of the stick like thick black veins.

"What is that?" I asked.

"A rattle stick. My grandmother made it. I'm going to rattle it while you play. So if you would. Like I showed you."

I beat on the drum, and the sound came out dead in that airless space.

"For God's sake," Lucy snapped. "Harder!" She had never been exceptionally friendly to me. But she'd been friendlier than this.

I slammed my hands down harder, and after a few beats, Lucy leaned back and nodded and watched. Not long after, she lifted her hand, stared at me as though daring me to stop her, and shook the stick. The sound it made was less rattle than buzz, as though it had wasps inside it. Lucy shook it a few more times, always at the same halfpause in my rhythm. Then her eyes rolled back in her head, and her spine arched, and my hand froze over the drum and Lucy snarled, "Don't stop."

After that, she began to chant. There was no tune to it, but a pattern, the pitch sliding up a little, down some, up a little more. When Lucy reached the top note, the ground under my crossed legs seemed to tingle, as though there were scorpions sliding out of the sand, but I didn't look down. I thought of the wooden figure behind me, but I didn't turn around. I played the drum, and I watched Lucy, and I kept my mouth shut.

We went on for a long, long time. After that first flush of fear, I was too mesmerized to think. My bones were tingling, too, and the air in the hogan was heavy. I couldn't get enough of it in my lungs. Tiny tidepools of sweat had formed in the hollow of Lucy's neck and under her ears and at the throat of her shirt. Under my palms, the drum was sweating, too, and the skin got slippery and warm. Not until Lucy stopped chanting did I realize that I was rocking side to side. Leaning.

"Want lunch?" Lucy said, standing and brushing the earth off her jeans.

I put my hands out perpendicular, felt the skin prickle and realized my wrists had gone to sleep even as they pounded out the rhythm Lucy had taught me. When I stood, the floor of the hogan seemed unstable, like the bottom of one of those balloon-tents my classmates sometimes had at birthday parties. I didn't want to look behind me, and then I did. The Dancing Man rocked slowly in no wind.

I turned around again, but Lucy had left the hogan. I didn't want to be alone in there, so I leapt through the hide curtain and winced against the sudden blast of sunlight and saw my grand-father.

He was propped in his wheelchair, positioned dead center

between the hogan and the back of his house. He must have been there the whole time, I thought, and somehow I'd managed not to notice him when I came in, because unless he'd gotten a whole lot better in the years since I'd seen him last, he couldn't have wheeled himself out. And he looked worse.

For one thing, his skin was falling off. At every exposed place on him, I saw flappy folds of yellow-pink. What was underneath was uglier still, not red or bleeding, just not skin. Too dry. Too colorless. He looked like a corn husk. An empty one.

Next to him on a rusty blue dolly, was a cylindrical silver oxygen tank. A clear tube ran from the nozzle at the top of the tank to the blue mask over my grandfather's nose and mouth. Above the mask, my grandfather's heavy-lidded eyes watched me, though they didn't seem capable of movement, either. Leave him out here, I thought, and those eyes would simply fill up with sand.

"Come in, Seth," Lucy told me, without any word to my grandfather or acknowledgment that he was there.

I had my hand on the screen door, was halfway into the house when I realized I'd heard him speak. I stopped. It had to have been him, I thought, and couldn't have been. I turned around and saw the back of his head tilting toward the top of the chair. Retracing my steps—I'd given him a wide berth—I returned to face him. The eyes stayed still, and the oxygen tank was silent. But the mask fogged, and I heard the whisper again.

"*Ruach,*" he said. It was what he always called me, when he called me anything.

In spite of the heat, I felt goosebumps spring from my skin, all along my legs and arms. I couldn't move. I couldn't answer. I should say hello, I thought. Say something.

I waited instead. A few seconds later, the oxygen mask fogged again. *"Trees,"* said the whisper-voice. *"Screaming. In the trees."* One of my grandfather's hands raised an inch or so off the arm of the chair and fell back into place.

"Patience," Lucy said from the doorway. "Come on, Seth." This time, my grandfather said nothing as I slipped past him into the house.

Lucy slid a bologna sandwich and a bag of Fritos and a plastic glass of apple juice in front of me. I lifted the sandwich, found that I couldn't imagine putting it in my mouth, and dropped it on the plate.

"Better eat," Lucy said. "We have a long day yet."

I ate, a little. Eventually, Lucy sat down across from me, but she didn't say anything else. She just gnawed a celery stick and watched the sand outside change color as the sun crawled west. The house was silent, the countertops and walls bare.

"Can I ask you something?" I finally asked.

Lucy was washing my plate in the sink. She didn't turn around, but she didn't say no.

"What are we doing? Out there, I mean."

No answer. Through the kitchen doorway, I could see my grandfather's living room, the stained wood floor and the single brown armchair lodged against a wall across from the TV. My grandfather had spent every waking minute of his life in this place for fifteen years or more, and there was no trace of him in it.

"It's a Way, isn't it?" I said, and Lucy shut off the water.

When she turned, her expression was the same as it had been all day, a little mocking, a little angry. She took a step toward the table.

"We learned about them at school," I said.

"Did you?"

"We're studying lots of Indian things."

The smile that spread over Lucy's face was cruel. Or maybe

just tired. "Good for you," she said. "Come on. We don't have much time."

"Is this to make my grandfather better?"

"Nothing's going to make your grandfather better." Without waiting for me, she pushed through the screen door into the heat.

This time, I made myself stop beside my grandfather's chair. I could just hear the hiss of the oxygen tank, like steam escaping from the boiling ground. When no fog appeared in the blue mask and no words emerged from the hiss, I followed Lucy into the hogan and let the hide curtain fall shut.

All afternoon and into the evening, I played the water drum while Lucy chanted. By the time the air began to cool outside, the whole hogan was vibrating, and the ground, too. Whatever we were doing, I could feel the power in it. I was the beating heart of a living thing, and Lucy was its voice. Once, I found myself wondering just what we were setting loose or summoning here, and I stopped, for a single beat. But the silence was worse. The silence was like being dead. And I thought I could hear the Dancing Man behind me. If I inclined my head, stopped playing for too long, I almost believed I'd hear him whispering.

When Lucy finally rocked to her feet and left without speaking to me, it was evening, and the desert was alive. I sat shaking as the rhythm spilled out of me and the sand soaked it up. Then I stood, and that unsteady feeling came over me again, stronger this time, as if the air were wobbling, too, threatening to slide right off the surface of the earth. When I emerged from the hogan, I saw black spiders on the wall of my grandfather's house, and I heard wind and rabbits and the first coyotes yipping somewhere to the west. My grandfather sat slumped in the same position he had been in hours and hours ago, which meant he had been baking out here all afternoon. Lucy was on the patio, watching the sun melt into the horizon's open mouth.

Her skin was slick, and her hair was wet where it touched her ear and neck.

"Your grandfather's going to tell you a story," she said, sounding exhausted. "And you're going to listen."

My grandfather's head rolled upright, and I wished we were back in the hogan, doing whatever it was we'd been doing. At least there, I was moving, pounding hard enough to drown sound out. Maybe. The screen door slapped shut, and my grandfather looked at me. His eyes were deep, deep brown, almost black, and horribly familiar. Did my eyes look like that?

"*Ruach,*" he whispered, and I wasn't sure, but his whisper seemed stronger than it had before. The oxygen mask fogged and stayed fogged. The whisper kept coming, as though Lucy had turned a spigot and left it open. "*You will know . . . Now . . . Then the world . . . won't be yours . . . anymore.*" My grandfather shifted like some sort of giant, bloated sand-spider in the center of its web, and I heard his ruined skin rustle. Above us, the whole sky went red.

"*At war's end . . .*" my grandfather hissed. "*Do you . . . understand?*" I nodded, transfixed. I could hear his breathing, now, the ribs rising, parting, collapsing. The tank machinery had gone strangely silent. Was he breathing on his own, I wondered? Could he, still?

"*A few days. Do you understand? Before the Red Army came . . .*" He coughed. Even his cough sounded stronger. "*The Nazis took . . . me. And the Gypsies. From . . . our camp. To Chelmno.*"

I'd never heard the word before. I've almost never heard it since. But as my grandfather said it, another cough roared out of his throat, and when it was gone, the tank was hissing again. Still, my grandfather continued to whisper.

"*To die. Do you understand?*" Gasp. Hiss. Silence. "*To die. But not yet. Not . . . right away.*" Gasp. "*We came . . . by train, but open train. Not cattle car. Wasteland. Farmland. Nothing. And then trees."* Under the mask, the lips twitched, and above it, the eyes closed completely. *"That first time. Ruach. All those . . . giant . . . green . . . trees. Unimaginable. To think anything . . . on the Earth we knew . . . could live that long."* His voice continued to fade, faster than the daylight. A few minutes more, I thought, and he'd be silent again, just machine and breath, and I could sit out here in the yard and let the evening wind roll over me.

"When they took . . . us off the train," my grandfather said, *"for one moment . . . I swear I smelled . . . leaves. Fat, green leaves . . . the new green . . . in them. Then the old smell . . . The only smell. Blood in dirt. The stink . . . of us. Piss. Shit. Open . . . sores. Skin on fire. Hnnn."* His voice trailed away, hardly-there air over barely moving mouth, and still he kept talking. *"Prayed for . . . some people . . . to die. They smelled . . . better. Dead. That was one prayer . . . always answered.*

"They took us . . . into the woods. Not to barracks. So few of them. Ten. Maybe twenty. Faces like . . . possums. Stupid. Blank. No thoughts. We came to . . . ditches. Deep. Like wells. Half full, already. They told us 'Stand still' . . . 'Breathe in.' "

At first, I thought the ensuing silence was for effect. He was letting me smell it. And I did smell it, the earth and the dead people, and there were German soldiers all around us, floating up out of the sand with black uniforms and white, blank faces. Then my grandfather crumpled forward, and I screamed for Lucy.

She came fast but not running and put a hand on my grandfather's back and another on his neck. After a few seconds, she straightened. "He's asleep," she told me. "Stay here." She wheeled my grandfather into the house, and she was gone a long time.

Sliding to a sitting position, I closed my eyes and tried not to hear my grandfather's voice. After a while I thought I could hear bugs and snakes and something larger padding out beyond the cacti. I could feel the moonlight, too, white and cool on my skin. The screen door banged, and I opened my eyes to find Lucy moving toward me, past me, carrying a picnic basket into the hogan.

"I want to eat out here," I said quickly, and Lucy turned with the hide curtain in her hand.

"Why don't we go in?" she said, and the note of coaxing in her voice made me nervous. So did the way she glanced over her shoulder into the hogan, as though something in there had spoken.

I stayed where I was, and eventually Lucy shrugged and let the curtain fall and dropped the basket at my feet. From the way she was acting, I thought she might leave me alone out there, but she sat down instead and looked at the sand and the cacti and the stars.

Inside the basket, I found warmed canned chili in a plastic Tupperware container and fry bread with cinnamon sugar and two cellophane-wrapped broccoli stalks that reminded me of uprooted miniature trees. In my ears, my grandfather's voice murmured, and to drown out the sound, I began to eat.

As soon as I was finished, Lucy began to stack the containers inside the basket, but she stopped when I spoke. "Please. Just talk to me a little."

She looked at me. The same look. As though we'd never even met. "Get some sleep. Tomorrow . . . well, let's just say tomorrow's a big day."

"For who?"

Lucy pursed her lips, and all at once, inexplicably, she seemed on the verge of tears. "Go to sleep."

"I'm not sleeping in the hogan," I told her.

"Suit yourself."

She was standing, and her back was to me now. I said, "Just tell me what kind of Way we're doing."

"An Enemy Way."

"What does it do?"

"It's nothing, Seth. God's sake. It's silly. Your grandfather thinks it will help him talk. He thinks it will sustain him while he tells you what he needs to tell you. Don't worry about the goddamn Way. Worry about your grandfather, for once."

My mouth flew open, and my skin stung as though she'd slapped me. I started to protest, then found I couldn't, and didn't want to. All my life, I'd built my grandfather into a figure of fear, a gasping, grotesque monster in a wheelchair. And my father had let me. I started to cry.

"I'm sorry," I said.

"Don't apologize to me." Lucy walked to the screen door.

"Isn't it a little late?" I called after her, furious at myself, at my father, at Lucy. Sad for my grandfather. Scared and sad.

One more time, Lucy turned around, and the moonlight poured down the white streaks in her hair like wax through a mold. Soon, I thought, she'd be made of it.

"I mean for my grandfather's Enemies," I said. "The Way can't really do anything to the Nazis. Right?"

"His Enemies are inside him," Lucy said, and left me.

For hours, it seemed, I sat in the sand, watching constellations explode out of the blackness, one after another, like firecrackers. In the ground, I heard night creatures stirring. I thought about the tube in my grandfather's mouth, and the unspeakable hurt in his eyes—because that's what it was, I thought now, not boredom, not hatred—and the enemies inside him. And then, slowly, exhaustion overtook me. The taste of fry bread lingered in my mouth, and the starlight got brighter still. I leaned back on my elbows. And finally, at God knows what hour,

I crawled into the hogan, under the tarpaulin canopy Lucy had made me, and fell asleep.

When I awoke, the Dancing Man was leaning over me on its branch, and I knew, all at once, where I'd seen eyes like my grandfather's, and the old fear exploded through me all over again. How had he done it, I wondered? The carving on the wooden man's face was basic, the features crude. But the eyes were his. They had the same singular, almost oval shape, with identical little notches right near the tear ducts. The same too-heavy lids. Same expression, or lack of any.

I was transfixed, and I stopped breathing. All I could see were those eyes dancing above me. When the Dancing Man was perfectly perpendicular, it seemed to stop momentarily, as though studying me, and I remembered something my dad had told me about wolves. "They're not trial-and-error animals," he'd said. "They wait and watch, wait and watch, until they're sure they know how the thing is done. And then they do it."

The Dancing Man went on weaving. First to one side, then the other, then back. Slower and slower. If it gets itself completely still, I thought—I *knew*—I would die. Or I would change. That was why Lucy was ignoring me. She had lied to me about what we were doing here. That was the reason they hadn't let my father stay. Leaping to my feet, I grabbed the Dancing Man around its clunky wooden base, and it came off the table with the faintest little suck, as though I'd yanked a weed out of the ground. I wanted to throw it, but I didn't dare. Instead, bent double, not looking at my clenched fist, I crab-walked to the entrance of the hogan, brushed back the hide curtain, slammed the Dancing Man down in the sand outside, and flung the curtain closed again. Then I squatted in the shadows, panting. Listening.

I crouched there a long time, watching the bottom of the curtain, expecting to see the Dancing Man slithering beneath it. But the hide stayed motionless, the hogan shadowy but still. I let myself sit back, and eventually, I slid into my sleeping bag again. I didn't expect to sleep anymore, but I did.

The smell of fresh fry bread woke me, and when I opened my eyes, Lucy was laying a tray of breads and sausage and juice on a woven red blanket on the floor of the hogan. My lips tasted sandy, and I could feel grit in my clothes and between my teeth and under my eyelids, as though I'd been buried overnight and dug up again.

"Hurry," Lucy told me, in the same chilly voice as yesterday.

I threw back the sleeping bag and started to sit up and saw the Dancing Man tilting on its branch, watching me. My whole body clenched, and I glared at Lucy and shouted, "How did that get back here?" Even as I said it, I realized that wasn't what I wanted to ask. More than how, I needed to know *when*. Exactly how long had it been hovering there without my knowing?

Without raising an eyebrow or even looking at me, Lucy shrugged and sat back. "Your grandfather wants you to have it," she said.

"I don't want it."

"Grow up."

Edging as far from the nightstand as possible, I shed the sleeping bag and sat down on the blanket and ate. Everything tasted sweet and sandy. My skin prickled with the intensifying heat. I still had a piece of fry bread and half a sausage left when I put my plastic fork down and looked at Lucy, who was arranging a new candle, settling the water drum near me, tying her hair back with a red rubber-band.

"Where did it come from?" I asked.

For the first time that day, Lucy looked at me, and this time, there really were tears in her eyes. "I don't understand your family," she said.

I shook my head. "Neither do I."

"Your grandfather's been saving that for you, Seth."

"Since when?"

"Since before you were born. Before your father was born. Before he ever imagined there could be a you."

This time, when the guilt came for me, it mixed with my fear rather than chasing it away, and I broke out sweating, and I thought I might be sick.

"You have to eat. Damn you," said Lucy.

I picked up my fork and squashed a piece of sausage into the fry bread and put it in my mouth. My stomach convulsed, but accepted what I gave it.

I managed a few more bites. As soon as I pushed the plate back, Lucy shoved the drum onto my lap. I played while she chanted, and the sides of the hogan seemed to breathe in and out, very slowly. I felt drugged. Then I wondered if I had been. Had they sprinkled something on the bread? Was that the next step? And toward what? Erasing me, I thought, almost chanted. Erasing me, and my hands flew off the drum, and Lucy stopped.

"Alright," she said. "That's probably enough." Then, to my surprise, she actually reached out and tucked some of my hair behind my ear, then touched my face for a second as she took the drum from me. "It's time for your Journey," she said.

I stared at her. The walls, I noticed, had stilled. I didn't feel any less strange, but a little more awake, at least. "Journey where?"

"You'll need water. And I've packed you a lunch." She slipped through the hide curtain, and I followed, dazed, and almost walked into my grandfather, parked right outside the hogan with a black towel on his head, so that his eyes and splitting skin were in shadow. He wore black leather gloves. His hands, I thought, must be on fire.

Right at the moment I noticed that Lucy was no longer with us, the hiss from the oxygen tank sharpened, and my grandfather's lips moved beneath the mask. *"Ruach."* This morning, the nickname sounded almost affectionate.

I waited, unable to look away. But the oxygen hiss settled again, like leaves after a gust of wind, and my grandfather said nothing more. A few seconds later, Lucy came back carrying a red backpack, which she handed to me.

"Follow the signs," she said, and turned me around until I was facing straight out from the road into the empty desert.

Struggling to life, I shook her hand off my shoulder. "Signs of what? What am I supposed to be doing?"

"Finding. Bringing back."

"I won't go."

"You'll go," Lucy said coldly. "The signs will be easily recognizable, and easy to locate. I have been assured of that. All you have to do is pay attention."

"Assured by who?"

"The first sign, I am told, will be left by the tall flowering cactus."

She pointed, which was unnecessary. A hundred yards or so from my grandfather's house, a spiky green cactus poked out of the rock and sand, supported on either side by two miniature versions of itself. A little cactus family, staggering in out of the waste.

I glanced at my grandfather under his mock-cowl, Lucy with her ferocious black eyes trained on me. Tomorrow, I thought, my father would come for me, and with any luck, I would never have to come out here again.

Then, suddenly, I felt ridiculous, and sad, and guilty once more.

Without even realizing what I was doing, I stuck my hand out and touched my grandfather's arm. The skin under his thin cotton shirt depressed beneath my fingers like the squishy center of a misshapen pillow. It wasn't hot. It didn't feel alive at all. I yanked my hand back, and Lucy glared at me. Tears sprang to my eyes.

"Get out of here," she said, and I stumbled away into the sand.

I don't really think the heat intensified as soon as I stepped away from my grandfather's house. But it seemed to. Along my bare arms and legs, I could feel the little hairs curling as though singed. The sun had scorched the sky white, and the only place to look that didn't hurt my eyes was down. Usually, when I walked in the desert, I was terrified of scorpions, but not that day. It was impossible to imagine anything scuttling or stinging or even breathing out there. Except me.

I don't know what I expected to find. Footprints, maybe, or animal scat, or something dead. Instead, stuck to the stem by a cactus needle, I found a yellow Post-It note. It said: "Pueblo."

Gently, avoiding the rest of the spiny needles, I removed the note. The writing was black and blocky. I glanced toward my grandfather's house, but he and Lucy were gone. The ceremonial hogan looked silly from this distance, like a little kid's pup tent.

Unlike the pueblo, I thought. I didn't even want to look that way, let alone go there. Already I could hear it, calling for me in a whisper that sounded far too much like my grandfather's. I could head for the road, I thought. Start toward town instead of the pueblo, and wait for a passing truck to carry me home. There would have to be a truck, sooner or later.

I did go to the road. But when I got there, I turned in the direction of the pueblo. I don't know why. I didn't feel as if I had a choice.

The walk, if anything, was too short. No cars passed. No road signs sprang from the dirt to point the way back to the world I knew. I watched the asphalt rise out of itself and roll in the heat, and I thought of my grandfather in the woods of Chelmno, digging graves in long green shadows. Lucy had put ice in the thermos she gave me, and the cubes clicked against my teeth when I drank. I walked, and I watched the desert, trying to spot a bird or a lizard. Even a scorpion would have been welcome. What I saw was sand, distant, colorless mountains, and white sky, a world as empty of life and its echoes as the surface of Mars, and just as red.

Even the lone road sign pointing to the pueblo was rusted through, crusted with sand, the letters so scratched away that the name of the place was no longer legible. I'd never seen a tourist here, or another living soul. Even calling it a pueblo seemed grandiose.

It was two sets of caves dug into the side of a cliff face, the top one longer than the bottom, so that together they formed a sort of gigantic cracked harmonica for the desert wind to play. The roof and walls of the top set of caves had fallen in. The whole structure seemed more monument than ruin, a marker of a people who no longer existed, rather than a place they had lived.

The bottom stretch of caves was largely intact, and as I stumbled toward them along the cracking macadam, I could feel their pull in my ankles. They seemed to be sucking the desert inside them, bit by bit. I stopped in front and listened.

I couldn't hear anything. I looked at the cracked, nearly square window openings, the doorless entryways leading into what had once been living spaces, the low, shadowed caves of dirt and rock. The whole pueblo just squatted there, inhaling sand through its dozens of dead mouths in a mockery of breath.

I waited a while longer, but the open air didn't feel any safer, just hotter. If my grandfather's Enemies were inside him, I suddenly wondered, and if we were calling them out, then where were they going? Finally I ducked through the nearest entryway and stood in the gloom.

After a few seconds, my eyes adjusted. But there was nothing to see. Along the window openings, blown sand lay in waves and mounds, like miniature relief maps of the desert outside. At my feet lay tiny stones, too small to hide scorpions, and a few animal bones, none of them larger than my pinky, distinguishable primarily by their curves, their stubborn whiteness.

Then, as though my entry had triggered some sort of mechanical magic show, sound coursed into my ears. In the walls, tiny feet and bellies slithered and scuttled. Nothing rattled a warning. Nothing hissed. And the footsteps, when they came, came so softly that at first I mistook them for sand shifting along the sills and the cool clay floor.

I didn't scream, but I staggered backward, lost my footing, slipped down, and I had the thermos raised and ready to swing when my father stepped out of the shadows and sat down cross-legged across the room from me.

"What—" I said, tears flying down my face, my heart thudding.

My father said nothing. From the pocket of his plain yellow button-up shirt, he pulled a packet of cigarette paper and a pouch of tobacco, then rolled a cigarette in a series of quick, expert motions.

"You don't smoke," I said, and my father lit the cigarette and dragged air down his lungs with a rasp.

"Far as you know," he answered. The orange glow from the tip looked like an open sore on his lips. Around us, the pueblo lifted, settled.

"Why does Grandpa call me '*Ruach*'?" I snapped. And still, my father only sat and smoked. The smell tickled unpleasantly in my nostrils. "God, Dad. What's going on? What are you doing here, and—"

"Do you know what *ruach* means?" he said.

I shook my head.

"It's a Hebrew word. It means ghost."

Hearing that was like being slammed to the ground. I couldn't get my lungs to work.

My father went on. "Sometimes, that's what it means. It depends what you use it with, you see? Sometimes, it means spirit, as in the spirit of God. Spirit of life. What God gave to his creations." He stubbed his cigarette in the sand, and the orange glow winked out like an eye blinking shut. "And sometimes it just means wind."

By my sides, I could feel my hands clutch as breath returned to my body. The sand felt cool and soft against my palms. "You don't know Hebrew, either," I said.

"I made a point of knowing that."

"Why?"

"Because that's what he called me, too," my father said, and rolled a second cigarette, but didn't light it. For a while, we sat. Then my father said, "Lucy called me two weeks ago. She told me it was time, and she said she needed a partner for your . . . ceremony. Someone to hide this, then help you find it. She said it was essential to the ritual." Reaching behind him, he produced a brown paper grocery bag with the top rolled down and tossed it to me. "I didn't kill it," he said.

I stared at him, and more tears stung my eyes. Sand licked along the skin of my legs and arms and crawled up my shorts and sleeves, as though seeking pores, points of entry. Nothing about my father's presence here was reassuring. Nothing about him had ever been reassuring, or anything else, I thought furiously, and the fury felt good. It helped me move. I yanked the bag to me.

The first thing I saw when I ripped it open was an eye. It was yellow-going-grey, almost dry. Not quite, though. Then I saw the folded, ridged black wings. A furry, broken body, twisted into a J. Except for the smell and the eye, it could have been a Halloween decoration.

"Is that a bat?" I whispered. Then I shoved the bag away and gagged.

My father glanced around at the walls, back at me. He made no move toward me. He was part of it, I thought wildly, he knew what they were doing, and then I pushed the thought away. It couldn't be true. "Dad, I don't understand," I pleaded.

"I know you're young," my father said. "He didn't do this to me until I left for college. But there's no more time, is there? You've seen him."

"Why do I have to do this at all?"

At that, my father's gaze swung down on me. He cocked his head and pursed his lips, as though I'd asked something completely incomprehensible. "It's your birthright," he said, and stood up.

We drove back to my grandfather's adobe in silence. The trip lasted less than five minutes. I couldn't even figure out what else to ask, let alone what I might do. I glanced at my father, wanting to scream at him, pound on him until he told me why he was acting this way.

Except that I wasn't sure he was acting anything but normal, for him. He didn't speak when he walked me to the ice-cream shop, either. When we arrived at the adobe, he leaned across me to push my door open, and I grabbed his hand.

"Dad. At least tell me what the bat is for."

My father sat up, moved the air-conditioning lever right, then hard back to the left, as though he could surprise it into working.

He always did this. It never worked. My father and his routines. "Nothing," he said. "It's a symbol."

"For what?"

"Lucy will tell you."

"But you know." I was almost snarling at him now.

"Only what Lucy told me. It stands for the skin at the tip of the tongue. It's the Talking God. Or associated with it. Or something. It goes where nothing else can go. Or helps someone else go there. I think. I'm sorry."

Gently, hand on my shoulder, he eased me out of the car before it occurred to me to wonder what he was apologizing for. But he surprised me by calling after me. "I promise you this, Seth. This is the last time in your life that you'll have to come here. Shut the door."

Too stunned and confused and scared to do anything else, I shut it, then watched as my father's car disintegrated into the first, far-off shadows of twilight. Already, too soon, I felt the change in the air, the night chill seeping through the gauze-dry day like blood through a bandage.

My grandfather and Lucy were waiting on the patio. She had her hand on his shoulder, her long hair gathered on her head, and without its dark frame, her face looked much older. And his—fully exposed now, without its protective shawl—looked like a rubber mask on a hook, with no bones inside to support it.

Slowly, my grandfather's wheelchair squeaked over the patio onto the hard sand as Lucy propelled it. I could do nothing but watch. The wheelchair stopped, and my grandfather studied me.

"*Ruach,*" he said. There was still no tone in his voice. But there were no holes in it, either, no gaps where last night his breath had failed him. "*Bring it to me.*"

It was my imagination, surely, or the first hint of breeze, that made the bag seem to squirm in my hands. This would be the last time, my father had said. I stumbled forward and dropped the paper bag in my grandfather's lap.

Faster than I'd ever seen him move, but still not fast, my grandfather crushed the bag against his chest. His head tilted forward, and I had the insane idea that he was about to sing to it, like a baby. But all he did was close his eyes and hold it.

"Alright, that's enough, I told you it doesn't work like that," Lucy said, and took the bag from him. She touched him gently on the back but didn't look at me.

"What did he just do?" I challenged her. "What did the bat do? Once more, Lucy smiled her slow, nasty smile. "Wait and see."

Then she was gone, and my grandfather and I were alone in the yard. The dark came drifting down the distant mountainsides like a fog bank, but faster. When it reached us, I closed my eyes and felt nothing except an instantaneous chill. I opened my eyes, and my grandfather was still watching me, head cocked a little on his neck. A wolf indeed.

"*Digging,*" he said. "*All we did, at first. Making pits deeper. The dirt so black. So soft. Like sticking your hands . . . inside an animal. All those trees leaning over us. Pines. Great white birches. Bark, smooth as baby skin. The Nazis gave . . . nothing to drink. Nothing to eat. But they paid . . . no attention, either. I sat next to the gypsy I had slept beside all . . . through the war. On a single slab of rotted wood. We had shared body heat. Blood from . . . each other's wounds. Infections. Lice.*

"*I never . . . even knew his name. Four years six inches from each other . . . never knew it. Couldn't understand each other. Never really tried. He'd saved—*" a cough rattled my grandfather's entire body, and his eyes got wilder, began to bulge, and I thought he wasn't breathing and almost yelled for Lucy again, but he gathered himself and went on. "*Buttons,*" he said. "*You understand? From somewhere. Rubbed their edges on rocks. Posts. Anything*

handy. Until they were . . . sharp. Not to kill. Not as a weapon."
More coughing. *"As a tool. To whittle."*
"Whittle," I said automatically, as though talking in my sleep.
*"When he was starving. When he . . . woke up screaming. When
we had to watch children's . . . bodies dangle from gallows . . . until
the first crows came for their eyes. When it was snowing, and . . .
we had to march . . . barefoot . . . or stand outside all night. The
gypsy whittled."*
Again, my grandfather's eyes ballooned in their sockets as
though they would burst. Again came the cough, shaking him so
hard that he almost fell from the chair. And again, he fought his
body to stillness.
"Wait," he gasped. *"You will wait. You must."*
I waited. What else could I do?
A long while later, he said, *"Two little girls."*
I stared at him. His words wrapped me like strands of a
cocoon. "What?"
*"Listen. Two girls. The same ones, over and over. That's what . . .
the gypsy . . . whittled."*
Dimly, in the part of my brain that still felt alert, I wondered
how anyone could tell if two figures carved in God knows what
with the sharpened edge of a button were the same girls.
But my grandfather just nodded. *"Even at the end. Even at
Chelmno. In the woods. In the moments . . . when we weren't digging, and the rest of us . . . sat. He went straight for the trees. Put
his hands on them like they were warm. Wept. First time, all war.
Despite everything we saw. Everything we knew . . . no tears from
him, until then. When he came back, he had . . . strips of pine bark
in his hands. And while everyone else slept . . . or froze . . . or died
. . . he worked. All night. Under the trees.*
*"Every few hours . . . shipments came. Of people, you under-
stand? Jews. We heard trains. Then, later, we saw creatures . . .*

between tree trunks. Thin. Awful. Like dead saplings walking. When the Nazis . . . began shooting . . . they fell with no sound. Poppoppop from the guns. Then silence. Things lying in leaves. In the wet.

"The killing wasn't . . . enough fun . . . for the Nazis, of course. They made us roll bodies . . . into the pits, with our hands. Then bury them. With our hands. Or our mouths. Sometimes our mouths. Dirt and blood. Bits of person in your teeth. A few of us laid down. Died on the ground. The Nazis didn't have . . . to tell us. We just . . . pushed anything dead . . . into the nearest pit. No prayers. No last look to see who it was. It was no one. Do you see? No one. Burying. Or buried. No difference.

"And still, all night, the gypsy whittled.

"For the dawn . . . shipment . . . the Nazis tried . . . something new. Stripped the newcomers . . . then lined them up . . . on the lip of a pit . . . twenty, thirty at a time. Then they played . . . perforation games. Shoot up the body . . . down it . . . see if you could get it . . . to flap apart . . . before it fell. Open up, like a flower.

"All through the next day. And all the next night. Digging. Waiting. Whittling. Killing. Burying. Over and over. Sometime . . . late second day, maybe . . . I got angry. Not at the Nazis. For what? Being angry at human beings . . . for killing . . . for cruelty . . . like being mad at ice, for freezing. It's just . . . what to expect. So I got angry . . . at the trees. For standing there. For being green, and alive. For not falling when bullets hit them.

"I started . . . screaming. Trying to. In Hebrew. In Polish. The Nazis looked up, and I thought they would shoot me. They laughed instead. One began to clap. A rhythm. See?"

Somehow, my grandfather lifted his limp hands from the arms of the wheelchair and brought them together. They met with a sort of crackle, like dry twigs crumbling.

"The gypsy . . . just watched. Still weeping. But also . . . after a while . . . nodding."

All this time, my grandfather's eyes had seemed to swell, as though there was too much air being pumped into his body. But now, the air went out of him in a rush, and the eyes went dark, and the lids came down. I thought maybe he'd fallen asleep again, the way he had last night. But I still couldn't move. Dimly, I realized that the sweat from my long day's walking had cooled on my skin, and that I was freezing.

My grandfather's lids opened, a little. He seemed to be peering at me from inside a trunk, or a coffin.

"I don't know how the gypsy knew . . . that it was ending. That it was time. Maybe just because . . . it had been hours . . . half a day . . . between shipments. The world had gone . . . quiet. Us. Nazis. Trees. Corpses. There had been worse places . . . I thought . . . to stop living. Despite the smell.

"Probably, I was sleeping. I must have been, because the gypsy shook me . . . by the shoulder. Then held out . . . what he'd made. He had it . . . balanced . . . on a stick he'd bent. So the carving moved. Back and forth. Up and down."

My mouth opened and then hung there. I was rock, sand, and the air moved through me and left me nothing.

"'Life,' the gypsy said to me, in Polish. First Polish I ever heard him speak. 'Life. You see?'

"I shook . . . my head. He said it again. 'Life.' And then . . . I don't know how . . . but I did . . . see.

"I asked him . . . 'Why not you?' He took . . . from his pocket . . . one of his old carvings. The two girls. Holding hands. I hadn't noticed . . . the hands before. And I understood.

"'My girls,' he said. Polish, again. 'Smoke. No more. Five years ago.' I understood that, too.

"I took the carving from him. We waited. We slept, side by side. One last time. Then the Nazis came.

"They made us stand. Hardly any of them, now. The rest gone.

Fifteen of us. Maybe less. They said something. German. None of us knew German. But to me . . . at least . . . the word meant . . . run.

"The gypsy . . . just stood there. Died where he was. Under the trees. The rest . . . I don't know. The Nazi who caught me . . . laughing . . . a boy. Not much . . . older than you. Laughing. Awkward with his gun. Too big for him. I looked at my hand. Holding . . . the carving. The wooden man. 'Life,' I found myself chanting . . . instead of Shema. 'Life.' Then the Nazi shot me in the head. Bang."

And with that single word, my grandfather clicked off, as though a switch had been thrown. He slumped in his chair. My paralysis lasted a few more seconds, and then I started waving my hands in front of me, as if I could ward off what he'd told me, and I was so busy doing that that I didn't notice, at first, the way my grandfather's torso heaved and rattled. Whimpering, I lowered my hands, but by then, my grandfather wasn't heaving anymore, and he'd slumped forward farther, and nothing on him was moving.

"*Lucy!*" I screamed, but she was already out of the house, wrestling my grandfather out of his chair to the ground. Her head dove down on my grandfather's as she shoved the mask up his face, but before their mouths even met, my grandfather coughed, and Lucy fell back, sobbing, tugging the mask back into place.

My grandfather lay where he'd been thrown, a scatter of bones in the dirt. He didn't open his eyes. The oxygen tank hissed, and the blue tube stretching to his mask filled with wet fog.

"How?" I whispered

Lucy swept tears from her eyes. "What?"

"He said he got shot in the head." And even as I said that, I felt it for the first time, that cold slithering up my intestines into my stomach, then my throat.

"Stop it," I said. But Lucy slid forward so that her knees were under my grandfather's head and ignored me. Overhead, I saw the moon half-embedded in the ridged black of the sky like the lidded eye of a gila monster. I stumbled around the side of the house, and without thinking about it, slipped into the hogan.

Once inside, I jerked the curtain down to block out the sight of Lucy and my grandfather and that moon, then drew my knees tight against my chest to pin that freezing feeling where it was. I stayed that way a long while, but whenever I closed my eyes, I saw people splitting open like peeled bananas, limbs strewn across bare black ground like tree branches after a lightning storm, pits full of naked dead people.

I'd wished him dead, I realized. At the moment he tumbled forward in his chair, I'd hoped he was dead. And for what, exactly? For being in the camps? For telling me about it? For getting sick, and making me confront it?

But with astonishing, disturbing speed, the guilt over those thoughts passed. And when it was gone, I realized that the cold had seeped down my legs and up to my neck. It clogged my ears, coated my tongue like a paste, sealing the world out. All I could hear was my grandfather's voice, like blown sand against the inside of my skull. *Life.* He was inside me, I thought. He had absorbed me, taken my place. He was becoming me.

I threw my hands over my ears, which had no effect. My thoughts flashed through the last two days, the drumming and chanting, the dead Talking God-bat in the paper bag, my father's good-bye, while that voice beat in my ears, attaching itself to my pulse. *Life.* And finally, I realized that I'd trapped myself. I was alone in the hogan in the dark. When I turned around, I would see the Dancing Man. It would be floating over me with its mouth wide open. And then it would be over, too late. It might already be.

Flinging my hands behind me, I grabbed the Dancing Man around its thin black neck. I could feel it bob on its branch, and I half-expected it to squirm as I fought to my feet. It didn't, but its wooden skin gave where I pressed it, like real skin. Inside my head, the new voice kept beating.

At my feet on the floor lay the matches Lucy had used to light her ceremonial candles. I snatched up the matchbook, then threw the carved thing to the ground, where it smacked on its base and tipped over, face up, staring at me. I broke a match against the matchbox, then another. The third match lit.

For one moment, I held the flame over the Dancing Man. The heat felt wonderful crawling toward my fingers, a blazing, living thing, chasing back the cold inside me. I dropped the match, and the Dancing Man disintegrated in a spasm of white orange flame.

And then, abruptly, there was nothing to be done. The hogan was a dirt-and-wood shelter, the night outside the plain old desert night, the Dancing Man a puddle of red and black ash I scattered with my foot. Still cold, but mostly tired, I staggered back outside and sat down hard against the side of the hogan and closed my eyes.

Footsteps woke me, and I sat up and found, to my amazement, that it was daylight. I waited, tense, afraid to look up, and then I did.

My father was kneeling beside me on the ground.

"You're here already?" I asked.

"Your grandpa died, Seth," he said. In his zombie-Dad voice, though he touched my hand the way a real father would. "I've come to take you home."

4

The familiar commotion in the hallway of the pension alerted me to my students' return. One of them, but only one, stopped outside my door. I waited, holding my breath, wishing I'd snapped out the light. But Penny didn't knock, and after a few seconds, I heard her careful, precise footfall continuing toward her room. And so I was alone with my puppets and my memories and my horrible suspicions, the way I have always been.

The way I am now, one month later, in my plain, posterless Ohio apartment with its cableless television and nearly bare cupboards and single shelf stacked with textbooks, on the eve of the new school year. I'm remembering rousing myself out of the malaise I couldn't quite seem to shake—have never, for one instant, shaken since—during that last ride home from my grandfather's. "I killed him," I told my father, and when he glanced at me, expressionless, I told him all of it, my grandfather's gypsy and the Dancing Man and the Way and the thoughts I'd had.

My father didn't laugh. He also didn't touch me. All he said was, "That's silly, Seth." And for a while, I thought it was.

But today, I am thinking of Rabbi Loew and his golem, the creature he infected with a sort of life. A creature that walked, talked, thought, saw, but couldn't taste. Couldn't feel. I'm thinking of my father, the way he always was. If I'm right, then of course it had been done to him, too. And I'm thinking of the way I only seem all the way real, even to me, when I see myself in the vividly reflective faces of my students.

It's possible, I realize, that nothing happened to me those last days at my grandfather's. It could have happened years before I was born. The gypsy had offered what he offered, and my grandfather had accepted, and as a result became what he was. Might have been. If that was true, then my father and I were unexceptional, in a way.

Natural progeny. We'd simply inherited our natures, and our limitations, the way all earthly creatures do.

But I can't help thinking about the graves I saw on this summer's trip, and the millions of people in them. And the millions more without graves. The ones who are smoke.

And I find that I can feel it, at last. Or that I've always felt it, without knowing what it was: the Holocaust, roaring down the generations like a wave of radiation, eradicating, in everyone it touches, the ability to trust people, experience joy, fall in love, believe in love when you see it in others.

And I wonder what difference it makes, in the end, whether it really was my grandfather, or the golem-grandfather that the gypsy made, who finally crawled out of the woods of Chelmno.

The Two Sams

for both of you

What wakes me isn't a sound. At first, I have no idea what it is: an earthquake, maybe; a vibration in the ground; a 2:00 A.M. truck shuddering along the switchback road that snakes up from the beach, past the ruins of the Baths, past the Cliff House and the automatons and coin machines chattering in the Musée Mécanique, past our apartment building until it reaches the flatter stretch of the Great Highway, which will return it to the saner neighborhoods of San Francisco. I lie still, holding my breath without knowing why. With the moon gone, the watery light rippling over the chipping bas-relief curlicues on our wall and the tilting, scuffed hardwood floor makes the room seem insubstantial, a projected reflection from the camera obscura perched on the cliffs a quarter mile away.

Then I feel it again, and I realize it's in the bed, not the ground. Right beside me. Instantly, I'm smiling. I can't help it. *You're playing on your own, aren't you?* That's what I'm thinking. Our first game. He sticks up a tiny fist, a twitching foot, a butt cheek, pressing against the soft roof and walls of his world, and I lay my palm against him, and he shoots off across the womb, curls in a far corner, waits. Sticks out a foot again.

The game terrified me at first. I kept thinking about signs in aquariums warning against tapping on glass, giving fish heart attacks. But he kept playing. And tonight, the thrum of his life is like magic fingers in the mattress, shooting straight up my spine into my shoulders, settling me, squeezing the terror out. Shifting the sheets softly, wanting Lizzie to sleep, I lean closer, and know, all at once, that this isn't what woke me.

For a split second, I'm frozen. I want to whip my arms around my head, ward them off like mosquitoes or bees, but I can't hear anything, not this time. There's just that creeping damp, the heaviness in the air like a fog bank forming. Abruptly, I dive forward and drop my head against the hot, round dome of Lizzie's stomach. Maybe I'm wrong, I think. I could be wrong. I press my ear against her skin, hold my breath, and for one horrible moment, I hear nothing at all, just the sea of silent amniotic fluid. I'm thinking about that couple, the Super Jews from our Bradley class who started coming when they were already seven months along. They came five straight weeks, and the woman would reach out sometimes, tug her husband's prayer curls, and we all smiled, imagining their daughter doing that, and then they weren't there anymore. The woman woke up one day and felt strange, empty, she walked around for hours that way and finally just got in her car and drove to the hospital and had her child, knowing it was dead.

But under my ear, something is moving, now. I can hear it inside my wife. Faint, unconcerned, unmistakable. Beat. Beat.

"Get out Tom's old records . . ." I sing, so softly, into Lizzie's skin. It isn't the song I used to use. Before, I mean. It's a new song. We do everything new, now. *"And he'll come dancing 'round."* It occurs to me that this song might not be the best choice, either. There are lines in it that could come back to haunt me, just the way the others have, the lines I never want to hear again and never even used to notice when I sang that song. They come creeping into my ears now, as though they're playing very quietly in a neighbor's room. *"I dreamed I held you. In my arms. When I awoke, dear. I was mistaken. And so I hung my head and I cried."* But then, I've found, that's the first great lesson of pregnancy: It all comes back to haunt you.

I haven't thought of this song, though, since the last time, I realize. Maybe they bring it with them?

Amidst the riot of thoughts in my head, a new one spins to the surface. Was it there the very first time? Did I feel the damp then? Hear the song? Because if I did, and I'm wrong . . .

I can't remember. I remember Lizzie screaming. The bathtub, and Lizzie screaming.

Sliding slowly back, I ease away toward my edge of the bed, then sit up, holding my breath. Lizzie doesn't stir, just lies there like the gut-shot creature she is, arms wrapped tight and low around her stomach, as though she could hold this one in, hold herself in, just a few days more. Her chin is tucked tight to her chest, dark hair wild on the pillow, bloated legs clamped around the giant blue cushion between them. Tip her upright, I think, and she'd look like a little girl on a hoppity horse. Then her kindergarten students would laugh at her again, clap and laugh when they saw her, the way they used to. Before.

For the thousandth time in the past few weeks, I have to quash an urge to lift her black-framed, square glasses from around her ears. She has insisted on sleeping with them since the day in March when the life inside her became—in the words of Dr. Seger, the woman Lizzie believes will save us—"viable," and the ridge in her nose is red and deep, now, and her eyes, always strangely small, seem to have slipped back in their sockets, as though cringing away from the unaccustomed closeness of the world, its unblurred edges. "The second I'm awake," Lizzie tells me savagely, the way she says everything these days, "I want to see."

"Sleep," I mouth, and it comes out a prayer.

Gingerly, I put my bare feet on the cold ground and stand. Always, it takes just a moment to adjust to the room. Because of the tilt of the floor—caused by the earthquake in '89—and the play of light over the walls and the sound of the surf and, sometimes, the seals out on Seal Rock and the litter of wood scraps and sawdust and half-built toys and menorahs and disemboweled clocks on every tabletop, walking through our apartment at night is like floating through a shipwreck.

Where are you? I think to the room and the shadows, turning in multiple directions as though my thoughts were a lighthouse beam. If they are, I need to switch them off. The last thing I want to provide, at this moment, for them, is a lure. Sweat breaks out on my back and legs as though I've been wrung. I don't want to breathe, don't want this infected air in my lungs, but I force myself. I'm ready. I have prepared this time. I'll do what I must if it's not too late and I get the chance.

"Where are you?" I whisper aloud, and something happens in the hall doorway. Not movement. Not anything I can explain. But I start over there, fast. It's much better if they're out there. "I'm coming," I say, and I'm out of the bedroom, pulling the door closed behind me as if that will help, and when I reach the living room, I consider snapping on the light but don't.

On the wall over the square, dark couch—we bought it dark, we were anticipating stains—the Pinocchio clock, first one I ever built, at age fourteen, makes its steady, hollow tock. It's all nose, that clock, which seems like such a bad idea, in retrospect. What was I saying, and to whom? *The hour is a lie. The room is a lie. Time is a lie.* "Gepetto," Lizzie used to call me before we were married, then after we were married, for a while, back when I used to show up outside her classroom door to watch her weaving between desks, balancing hamsters and construction paper and graham crackers and half-pint milk cartons in her arms while kindergartners nipped between and around her legs like ducklings.

Gepetto. Who tried so hard to make a living boy.

Tock.

"Stop," I snap to myself and the leaning walls. There is less damp here. They're somewhere else.

The first tremble comes as I return to the hall. I clench my knees and shoulders, willing myself still. As always, the worst thing about the trembling and the sweating is the confusion that causes them. I can never decide if I'm terrified or elated. Even before I realized what was happening, there was a kind of elation.

Five steps down the hall, I stop at the door to what was once our workshop, housing my building area and Lizzie's cut-and-paste table for classroom decorations. It has not been a workshop for almost four years now. For four years, it has been nothing at all. The knob is just a little wet when I slide my hand around it, the hinges silent as I push open the door.

"Okay," I half-think, half-say, trembling, sliding into the room and shutting the door behind me. "It's okay." Tears leap out of my lashes as though they've been hiding there. It doesn't feel as if I actually cried them. I sit down on the bare floor, breathe, and stare around the walls, also bare. One week more. Two weeks, tops. Then, just maybe, the crib, fully assembled, will burst from the closet, the dog-cat carpet will unroll itself like a Torah scroll over the hardwood, and the mobiles Lizzie and I made together will spring from the ceiling like streamers. *Surprise!*

The tears feel cold on my face, uncomfortable, but I don't wipe them. What would be the point? I try to smile. There's a part of me, a small, sad part, that feels like smiling. "Should I tell you a bedtime story?"

I could tell about the possum. We'd lost just the one, then, and more than a year had gone by, and Lizzie still had moments, seizures, almost, when she ripped her glasses off her face in the middle of dinner and hurled them across the apartment and jammed herself into the kitchen corner behind the stacked washer-dryer unit. I'd stand over her and say, "Lizzie, no," and try to fight what I was feeling, because I didn't like that I was feeling it. But the more often this happened, and it happened a lot, the angrier I got. Which made me feel like such a shit.

"Come on," I'd say, extra gentle, to compensate, but of course I didn't fool her. That's the thing about Lizzie. I knew it when I married her, even loved it in her: She recognizes the worst in people. She can't help it. And she's never wrong about it.

"You don't even care," she'd hiss, her hands snarled in her twisting brown hair as though she was going to rip it out.

"Fuck you, of course I care."

"It doesn't mean anything to you."

"It means what it means. It means we tried, and it didn't work, and it's awful, and the doctors say it happens all the time, and we need to try again. It's awful but we have to deal with it, we have no choice if we want—"

"It means we lost a child. It means our child died. You asshole!"

Once—one time—I handled that moment right. I looked down at my wife, my playmate since junior high, the perpetually sad person I made happy sometimes, and who made everyone around her happy even though she was sad, and I saw her hands twist harder in her hair, and I saw her shoulders cave in toward her knees, and I just blurted it out.

"You look like a lint ball," I told her.

Her face flew off her chest, and she glared at me. Then she threw her arms out, not smiling, not free of anything, but wanting me with her. Down I came. We were lint balls together.

Every single other time, I blew it. I stalked away, or I started to cry, or I fought back.

"Let's say that's true," I'd say. "We lost a child. I'll admit it, I can see how one could choose to see it that way. But I don't feel that. By the grace of God, it doesn't quite feel like that to me."

"That's because it wasn't *inside* you."

"That's such—" I'd start, then stop, because I didn't really think it was. And that wasn't what I was trying to say, anyway.

"Lizzie. God. I'm just . . . I'm trying to do this well. I'm trying to get us to the place where we can try again. Where we can have a child. One that lives. Because that's the point, isn't it? That's the ultimate goal?"

"Honey, this one just wasn't meant to be," Lizzie would sneer, imitating her mom, or maybe my mom, or any one of a dozen people we knew. "Is that what you want to say next?"

"You know it isn't."

"How about, *The body knows. Something just wasn't right. These things do happen for a reason.*"

"Lizzie, stop."

"Or, Years from now, you'll look at your child, your living, breathing, beautiful child, and you'll realize that you wouldn't have had him or her if the first one had survived. There'd be a completely different creature there. How about that one?"

"Lizzie, Goddammit. Just shut up. I'm saying none of those things, and you know it. I'm saying I wish this had never happened. And now that it has happened, I want it to be something that happened in the past. Because I still want to have a baby with you."

Usually, most nights, she'd stand up, then. I'd pick up her glasses from wherever she'd thrown them and hand them to her, and she'd fix them on her face and blink as the world rushed forward. Then she'd look at me, not unkindly. More than once, I'd thought she was going to touch my face or my hand.

Instead, what she said was, "Jake. You have to understand." Looking through her lenses at those moments was like peering through a storm window, something I would never again get open, and through it I could see the shadows of everything Lizzie carried with her and could not bury and didn't seem to want to. "Of all the things that have happened to me. All of them. You're probably the best. And this is the worst."

Then she'd step around me, around the dinner table, and go to bed. And I'd go out to walk, past the Cliff House, past the Musée, sometimes all the way down to the ruins of the Baths, where I'd stroll along the crumbling concrete walls that had once framed the largest public bathing pool in the United States and now framed nothing but marsh grass and drain water and echo. Sometimes the fog would roll over me, a long, gray ghost-tide, and I'd float off on it, in it, just another trail of living vapor combing the earth in search of a world we'd all gotten the idea was here somewhere. Where, I wonder, had that idea come from, and how did so many of us get it?

"But that isn't what you want to hear," I say suddenly to the not-quite-empty workroom, the cribless floor. "Is it?" For a second, I panic, fight down the urge to leap to my feet and race for Lizzie. If they've gone back in there, then I'm too late, anyway. And if they haven't, my leaping about just might scare them in that direction. In my head, I'm casting around for something to say that will hold them while I swing my gaze back and forth, up to the ceiling and down again.

"I was going to tell you about the possum, right? One night, maybe eight months or so after you were . . ." The word curls on my tongue like a dead caterpillar. I say it anyway. "Born." Nothing screams in my face or flies at me, and my voice doesn't break. And I think there might have been a flutter across the room, something other than the curtains. I have to believe there was. And the damp is still in here.

"It was pretty amazing," I say fast, staring at where the flutter was, as though I could pin it there. "Lizzie kicked me and woke me up. 'You hear that?' she asked. And of course I did. Fast, hard scrabbling, click-click-click, from right in here. We came running and saw a tail disappear behind the dresser. There was a dresser, then, I made it myself. The drawers came out sideways and the handles formed kind of a pumpkin face, just for fun, you know? Anyway, I got down on my hands and knees and found this huge white possum staring right at me. I didn't even know there were possums here. This one took one look at me and keeled over with its feet in the air. Playing dead."

I throw myself on the ground with my feet in the air. It's like a memory, a dream, a memory of a dream, but I half-believe I feel a weight on the soles of my feet, as though something had climbed onto them, for a ride, maybe.

"I got a broom. Your . . . Lizzie got a trash can. And for the next, I don't know, three hours, probably, we chased this thing around and around the room. We had the windows wide open. All it had to do was hop up and out. Instead, it hid behind the dresser, playing dead, until I poked it with the broom, and then it would race along the baseboard or into the middle of the room and flip on its back again, as if to say okay, now I'm really dead, and we couldn't get it to go up and out. We couldn't get it to do anything but die. Over and over and over. And—"

I stop, lower my legs abruptly, and sit up. I don't say the rest. How, at 3:45 in the morning, Lizzie dropped the trash can to the floor, looked at me, and burst out crying. Threw her glasses at the wall and broke one of the lenses and wept while I stood there, so tired, with this possum belly-up at my feet and the sea air flooding the room. We'd been laughing, until then. I could hardly stand up for exhaustion, and I'd loved laughing with Lizzie so goddamn much.

"Lizzie," I'd said. "I mean, fuck. Not everything has to relate to that. Does it? Does everything we ever think or do, for the rest of our lives . . ." But of course, it does. I think I even knew that then. And that was after only one.

"Would you like to go for a walk?" I say carefully, clearly, because this is it. The only thing I can think of, and therefore the only chance we have. How does one get a child to listen, really? I wouldn't know. "We'll go for a stroll, okay? Get nice and sleepy?" I still can't see anything. Most of the other times, I've caught half a glimpse, at some point, a trail of shadow. Turning, leaving the door cracked open behind me, I head for the living room. I slide my trench coat over my boxers and Green Apple T-shirt, slip my tennis shoes onto my bare feet. My ankles will be freezing. In the pocket of my coat, I feel the matchbook I left there, the single tiny silver key. It has been two months, at least, since the last time they came, or at least since they let me know it. But I have stayed ready.

As I step onto our stoop, wait a few seconds, and pull the door closed, I am flooded with sensory memory—it's like being dunked—of the day I first became aware. Over two years ago, now. Over a year after the first one. Halfway to dreaming, all but asleep, I was overcome by an overwhelming urge to put my ear to Lizzie's womb and sing to the new tenant in there. Almost six weeks old, at that point. I imagined seeing through my wife's skin, watching toe and finger shapes forming in the red, waving wetness like lines on an Etch-A-Sketch.

"You are my sun—" I started, and knew, just like that, that something else was with me. There was the damp, for one thing, and an extra soundlessness in the room, right beside me. I can't explain it. The sound of someone else listening.

I reacted on instinct, shot upright and accidentally yanked all the blankets off Lizzie and shoved my arms at where the presence seemed to be, and Lizzie blinked awake and narrowed her spectacleless eyes at the shape of me, the covers twisted on the bed.

"There's something here," I babbled, pushing with both hands at the empty air.

Lizzie just squinted, coolly. Finally, after a few seconds, she snatched one of my waving hands out of the air and dropped it against her belly. Her skin felt smooth, warm. My forefinger slipped into her belly button, felt the familiar knot of it, and I found myself aroused. Terrified, confused, ridiculous, and aroused.

"It's just Sam," she said, stunning me. It seemed impossible that she was going to let me win that fight. Then she smiled, pressing my hand to the second creature we had created together. "You and me and Sam." She pushed harder on my hand, slid it down her belly toward the center of her.

We made love, held each other, sang to her stomach. Not until long after Lizzie had fallen asleep, just as I was finally dropping off, did it occur to me that she could have been more right than she knew. Maybe it was just us, and Sam. The first Sam— the one we'd lost—returning to greet his successor with us.

Of course, he hadn't come just to listen or to watch. But how could I have known that, then? And how did I know that that was what the presence was, anyway? I didn't. And when it came back late the next night, with Lizzie this time sound asleep and me less startled, I slid aside to make room for it so we could both hear. Both whisper.

Are both of you with me now, I wonder? I'm standing on my stoop and listening, feeling, as hard as I can. Please, God, let them be with me. Not with Lizzie. Not with the new one. That's the only name we have allowed ourselves this time. The new one.

"Come on," I say to my own front door, to the filigrees of fog that float forever on the air of Sutro Heights, as though the atmosphere itself has developed bas-relief and gone art deco. "Please. I'll tell you a story about the day you were born."

I start down the warped, wooden steps toward our garage. Inside my pocket, the little silver key darts between my fingers, slippery and cool as a minnow. In my mouth, I taste the fog and the perpetual garlic smell from the latest building to perch at the jut of the cliffs and call itself the Cliff House—the preceding three all collapsed or burned to the ground—and something else, too. I realize, finally, what it is, and the tears come flooding back.

What I'm remembering, this time, is Washington D.C., the grass brown and dying in the blazing August sun as we raced down the Mall from museum to museum in a desperate, headlong hunt for cheese. We were in the ninth day of the ten-day tetracycline program Dr. Seger had prescribed, and Lizzie just seemed tired, but I swear I could feel the walls of my intestines, raw and sharp and scraped clean, the way teeth feel after a particularly vicious visit to the dentist. I craved milk, and got nauseous just thinking about it. Drained of its germs, its soft, comforting skin of use, my body felt skeletal, a shell without me in it.

That was the point, as Dr. Seger explained it to us. We'd done our Tay-Sachs, tested for lead, endured endless blood screenings to check on things like prolactin, lupus anticoagulant, TSH. We would have done more tests, but the doctors didn't recommend them, and our insurance wouldn't pay. "A couple of miscarriages, it's really not worth intensive investigation." Three different doctors told us that. "If it happens a couple more times, we'll know something's really wrong."

Dr. Seger had a theory, at least, involving old bacteria lingering in the body for years, decades, tucked up in the fallopian tubes or hidden in the testicles or just adrift in the blood, riding the heart current in an endless, mindless, circle. "The mechanism of creation is so delicate," she told us. "So efficiently, masterfully created. If anything gets in there that shouldn't be, well, it's like a bird in a jet engine. Everything just explodes."

How comforting, I thought but didn't say at that first consultation, because when I glanced at Lizzie, she looked more than comforted. She looked hungry, perched on the edge of her chair with her head half over Dr. Seger's desk, so pale, thin, and hard, like a starved pigeon being teased with crumbs. I wanted to grab her hand. I wanted to weep.

As it turns out, Dr. Seger may have been right, or maybe we got lucky this time. Because that's the thing about miscarriage: three thousand years of human medical science, and no one knows any fucking thing at all. It just happens, people say, like a bruise or a cold. And it does, I suppose. Just happen, I mean. But not like a cold. Like dying. Because that's what it is.

So for ten days, Dr. Seger had us drop tetracycline tablets down our throats like depth charges, blasting everything living inside us out. And on that day in D.C.—we were visiting my cousin, the first time I'd managed to coax Lizzie anywhere near extended family since all this started—we'd gone to the Holocaust Museum, searching for anything strong enough to take our minds off our hunger, our desperate hope that we were scoured, healthy, clean. But it didn't work. So we went to the Smithsonian. And three people from the front of the ticket line, Lizzie suddenly grabbed my hand, and I looked at her, and it was the old Lizzie or the ghost of her, eyes flashing under their black rims, smile instantaneous, shockingly bright.

"Dairy," she said. "Right this second."

It took me a breath to adjust. I hadn't seen my wife this way in a long, long while, and as I stared, the smile slipped on her face. With a visible effort, she pinned it back in place. "Jake. Come on."

None of the museum cafés had what we wanted. We paid admission and went racing past sculptures and animal dioramas and parchment documents to the cafés, where we stared at yogurt in plastic containers—but we didn't dare eat yogurt—and cups of tapioca that winked, in our fevered state, like the iced-over surfaces of Canadian lakes. But none of it would have served. We needed a cheddar wheel, a lasagna we could scrape free of pasta and tomatoes so we could drape our tongues in strings of crusted mozzarella. What we settled for, finally, was four giant bags of generic cheese puffs from a 7-Eleven. We sat together on the edge of a fountain and stuffed each other's mouths like babies, like lovers.

It wasn't enough. The hunger didn't abate in either of us. Sometimes I think it hasn't since.

God, it was glorious, though. Lizzie's lips around my orange-stained fingers, that soft, gorgeous crunch as each individual puff popped apart in our mouths, dusting our teeth and throats while spray from the fountain brushed our faces and we dreamed separate, still-hopeful dreams of children.

And that, in the end, is why I have to, you see. My two Sams. My lost loved ones. Because maybe what everyone says is true. It doesn't seem like it could be, but maybe it is. Maybe, mostly, miscarriage just happens. And then, for most couples, it just stops happening one day. And afterward—if only because there isn't time—you start to forget. Not what happened. Not what was lost. But what the loss meant, or at least what it felt like. I've come to believe that time alone won't swallow grief, or heal a marriage. But perhaps filled time . . .

In my pocket, my fingers close over the silver key, and I take a deep breath of the damp in the air, which is mostly just Sutro Heights damp now that we're outside. We have always loved it here, Lizzie and I. In spite of everything, we can't bring ourselves to leave. "Let me show you," I say, trying not to plead. I've taken too long, I think. They've gotten bored. They'll go back in the house. I lift the ancient, rusted padlock on our garage door, tilt it so I can see the slot in the moonlight, and slide the key home.

It has been months since I've been out here—we use the garage for storage, not for our old Nova—and I've forgotten how heavy the salt-saturated wooden door is. It comes up with a creak, slides over my head and rocks unsteadily in its runners. How, I'm thinking, did I first realize that the presence in our room was our first, unborn child? The smell, I guess, like an unripe lemon, fresh and sour all at once. Lizzie's smell. Or maybe it was the song springing unbidden, over and over, to my lips. *"When I awoke, dear, I was mistaken."* Those things, and the fact that now, these last times, they both seem to be there.

The first thing I see once my eyes adjust is my grandfather glaring out of his portrait at me, his hair thread-thin and wild on his head like a spiderweb swinging free, his lips flat, crushed together, his outsized, lumpy potato of a body under his perpetually half-zipped judge's robes. And there are his eyes, one blue, one green, which he once told me allowed him to see 3-D, before I knew that everyone could. A children's-rights activist before there was a name for such things, a three-time candidate for a state bench seat and three-time loser, he'd made an enemy of his daughter—my mother—by wanting a son so badly. And he'd made a disciple out of me by saving Lizzie's life. Turning her father in to the cops, then making sure that he got thrown in jail, then forcing both him and his whole family into counseling, getting him work when he got out, checking in on him every single night, no matter what, for six years, until Lizzie was away and free. Until eight months ago, on the day Dr. Seger confirmed that we were pregnant for the third time, his portrait hung beside the Pinocchio clock on the living-room wall. Now it lives here. One more casualty.

"Your namesake," I say to the air, my two ghosts. But I can't take my eyes off my grandfather. Tonight is the end for him, too, I realize. The real end, where the ripples his life created in the world glide silently to stillness. Could you have seen them, I want to ask, with those 3-D eyes that saw so much? Could you have saved them? Could you have thought of another, better way? Because mine is going to hurt. "His name was Nathan, really. But he called us 'Sam.' Your mother and me, we were both 'Sam.' That's why—"

That's why Lizzie let me win the argument over still naming the second child Sam. Not because she'd let go of the idea that the first one had to have a name, was a specific living creature, a child of ours. But because she'd rationalized. Sam was to be the name, male or female. So whatever the first child had been, the second would be the other. Would have been. *You see, Lizzie,* I think to the air, wanting to punch the walls of the garage, scream to the cliffs, break down in sobs. *You think I don't know. But I do.*

If we survive this night, and our baby is still with us in the morning, and we get to meet him someday soon, he will not be named Sam. He won't be Nathan, either. My grandfather would have wanted Sam.

I force myself toward the back of the garage. There's no point in drawing this out, surely. Nothing to be gained. But at the door to the meat freezer, where the game hunter who rented our place before us stored his waxed-paper packets of venison and elk, I suddenly stop.

I can feel them. They're still here. They have not gone back to Lizzie. They are not hunched near her navel, whispering their terrible, soundless whispers. That's how I imagine it happening, only it doesn't feel like imagining. And it isn't all terrible. I swear I heard it happen to the second Sam. The first Sam would wait, watching me, hovering near the new life in Lizzie like a hummingbird near nectar, then darting forward when I backed away and singing a different sort of song, of a whole other world, parallel to ours, free of terrors or at least this terror, the one that just plain living breeds in everything alive. Maybe that world we're all born dreaming really does exist, but the only way to reach it is through a trapdoor in the womb. Maybe it's better where my children are. God, I want it to be better.

"You're by the notebooks," I say, and almost smile as my hand slides volitionlessly from the handle of the freezer door and I stagger toward the boxes stacked up, haphazard, along the back wall. The top one on the nearest stack is open slightly, its cardboard damp and reeking when I peel the flaps all the way back.

There they are. The plain, perfect-bound school-composition notebooks Lizzie bought as diaries to chronicle the lives of her first two children in the 280 or so days before we were to know them. "I can't look in those," I say aloud, but I can't help myself. I lift the top one from the box, place it on my lap, and sit down. It's my imagination, surely, that weight on my knees, as though something else has just slid down against me. Like a child, to look at a photo album. *Tell me, Daddy, about the world without me in it.* Suddenly, I'm embarrassed. I want to explain. That first notebook, the other one, is almost half my writing, not just Lizzie's. But this one . . . I was away, Sam, on a selling trip, for almost a month. And when I came back . . . I couldn't. Not right away. I couldn't even watch your mom doing it. And two weeks later . . .

"The day you were born," I murmur, as if it were a lullaby, "we went to the redwoods, with the Giraffes." Whatever it is, that weight on me, shifts a little. Settles. "That isn't really their name, Sam. Their name is Girard. 'Giraffe' is what you would have called them, though. They would have made you. They're so tall. So funny. They would have put you on their shoulders to touch EXIT signs and ceiling tiles. They would have dropped you upside down from way up high and made you scream.

"This was December, freezing cold, but the sun was out. We stopped at a gas station on our way to the woods, and I went to get Bugles, because that's what Giraffes eat—the ones we know, anyway. Your mom went to the restroom. She was in there a long time. And when she came out, she just looked at me. And I knew."

My fingers have pushed the notebook open, pulled the pages apart. They're damp, too. Half of them are ruined, the words in multicolored inks like pressed flowers on the pages, smeared out of shape, though their meaning remains clear.

"I waited. I stared at your mother. She stared at me. Joseph—Mr. Giraffe—came in to see what was taking so long. Your mom just kept on staring. So I said, 'Couldn't find the Bugles.' Then I grabbed two bags of them, turned away, and paid. And your mom got in the van beside me, and the Giraffes put on their bouncy, happy, Giraffe music, and we kept going.

"When we got to the woods, we found them practically empty, and there was this smell, even though the trees were dead. It wasn't like spring. You couldn't smell pollen or see buds, there was just the sunlight and bare branches and this mist floating up and catching on the branches and forming shapes like the ghosts of leaves. I tried to hold your mother's hand, and she let me at first. And then she didn't. She disappeared into the mist. The Giraffes had to go find her in the end, when it was time to go home. It was almost dark as we got in the van, and none of us were speaking. I was the last one in. And all I could think, as I took my last breath of that air, was, *Can you see this? Did you see the trees, my sweet son, daughter or son, on your way out of the world?*

Helpless, now, I drop my head, bury it in the wet air as though there were a child's hair there, and my mouth is moving, chanting the words in the notebook on my lap. I read them only once, on the night Lizzie wrote them, when she finally rolled over, with no tantrum, no more tears, nothing left, closed the book against her chest, and went to sleep. But I remember them still. There's a sketch, first, what looks like an acorn with a dent in the top. Next to it Lizzie has scrawled, *You. Little rice-bean.* On the day before it died. Then there's the list, like a rosary: *I'm so sorry. I'm so sorry I don't get to know you. I'm so sorry for wishing this was over, now, for wanting the bleeding to stop. I'm so sorry that I will never have the chance to be your mother. I'm so sorry you will never have the chance to be in our family. I'm so sorry that you are gone.*

I recite the next page, too, without even turning to it. The *I-don't-wants: a D&C; a phone call from someone who doesn't know, to ask how I'm feeling; a phone call from someone who does, to ask how I am; to forget this, ever; to forget you.*

And then, at the bottom of the page: *I love fog. I love seals. I love the ghosts of Sutro Heights. I love my mother, even though. I love Jake. I love having known you. I love having known you. I love having known you.*

With one long, shuddering breath, as though I'm trying to slip out from under a sleeping cat, I straighten my legs, lay the notebook to sleep in its box, tuck the flaps around it, and stand. It's time. Not past time, just time. I return to the freezer and flip the heavy white lid.

The thing is, even after I looked in here, the same day I brought my grandfather's portrait out and wound up poking around the garage, lifting box tops, touching old, unused bicycles and cross-country skis, I would never have realized. If she'd done the wrapping in waxed paper, laid it all in the bottom of the freezer, I would have assumed it was meat, and I would have left it there. But Lizzie is Lizzie, and instead of waxed paper, she'd used red and blue construction paper from her classroom, folded the paper into perfect squares with perfect corners, and put a single star on each of them. So I lifted them out, just as I'm doing now.

They're so cold cradled against me. The red package. The blue one. So light. The most astounding thing about the wrapping, really, is that she managed it at all. How do you get paper and tape around nothing and get it to hold its shape? From another nearby box, I lift a gold and green blanket. I had it on my bottom bunk when I was a kid. The first time Lizzie lay on my bed—without me in it, she was just lying there—she wrapped herself in this. I spread it now on the cold cement floor and gently lay the packages down.

In Hebrew, the word for miscarriage translates, literally, as *something dropped*. It's no more accurate a term than any of the others humans have generated for the whole, apparently incomprehensible process of reproduction, right down to *conception*. Is that what we do? Conceive? Do we literally dream our children? Is it possible that miscarriage, finally, is just waking up to the reality of the world a few months too soon?

Gently, with the tip of my thumbnail, I slit the top of the red package and fold it open. It comes apart like origami, so perfect, arching back against the blanket. I slit the blue package and pull back its flaps, widening the opening. One last parody of birth.

How did she do it, I wonder? The first time, we were home, she was in the bathroom. She had me bring Ziploc baggies and ice. *For testing*, she said. *They'll need it for testing*. But they'd taken it for testing. How had she gotten it back? And the second one had happened—finished happening—in a gas-station bathroom somewhere between the Golden Gate Bridge and the Muir Woods. And she'd said nothing, asked for nothing.

"Where did she keep you?" I murmur, staring down at the formless red and gray spatters, the bunched-up tissue that might have been tendon or skin one day. Sam, one day. In the red package, there is more, a hump of frozen something with strings of red spiraling out from it, sticking to the paper, like the rays of an imploding sun. In the blue package, there are some red dots and a few strands of filament. Virtually nothing.

The song comes, and the tears with them. *You'll never know. Dear. How much I love you. Please don't take. Please don't take.* I think of my wife upstairs in our life, sleeping with her arms around her child. The one that won't be Sam, but just might live.

The matches slide from my pocket. Pulling one out of the little book is like ripping a blade of grass from the ground. I scrape it to life, and its tiny light warms my hand, floods the room, flickering as it sucks the oxygen out of the damp. Will this work? How do I know? For all I know, I am imagining it all. The miscarriages were bad luck, hormone deficiencies, a virus in the blood, and the grief that got in me was at least as awful as what got in Lizzie, it just lay dormant longer. And now it has made me crazy.

But if it is better where you are, my Sams. And if you're here to tell the new one about it, to call him away . . .

"The other night, dear," I find myself saying, and then I'm singing it like a Shabbat blessing, a Hanukkah song, something you offer to the emptiness of a darkened house to keep the dark and emptiness back one more week, one more day. *"As I lay sleeping. I dreamed I held you. In my arms."*

I lower the match to the red paper, then the blue, and as my children melt, become dream once more, I swear I hear them sing to me.

Acknowledgments

Most of these stories evolved over the past ten years, and were retold on numerous occasions before I even considered writing them down. As a result, I have had the benefit of invaluable input and support from many people.

My students, first of all, have never been shy about letting me know when I'd stopped scaring (or even amusing) them, and they have also filled my life with stories. The wise and talented Jennifer Revelle—medievalist, lawyer-to-be, triathlete, friend—has been a particular help, goading and harassing and encouraging me since taking the first class I ever taught and pointing out that I shared my detached earlobes with an ungodly percentage of the world's known serial killers. Barbara and Christopher Roden inspire many through their superb work with the Ghost Story Society and Ash-Tree Press, and in 1998, they took a chance on an absurdly long story by a completely unknown writer and welcomed me into a whole new world. Stephen Jones has done much to introduce me and so many other writers to the speculative fiction community. Kelly Link has proven almost as much fun to know and work with as she is to read. And while I'm grateful to Ramsey Campbell for his introduction to this book, I'm more grateful for the decades of truly unpleasant nights he has given me since I started reading him at age eight. In some ways, these stories are his fault.

Both Kathy Anderson, my agent, and Tina Pohlman, my very

fine editor at Carroll & Graf, have rolled gracefully with the capricious whims of my writing nature, and both remain sources of essential insight and wisdom. Many thanks, too, to Wendie Carr and Herman Graf for their tireless work and fine taste in desserts.

I am especially indebted to Ellen Datlow, who has not only encouraged my work but has been extraordinarily generous and helpful in her support of it ever since I met her.

Finally, as always, I want to thank my wife Kim for being herself, and for never letting these stories be less than they could be.